CW00664303

RUNNING: CARUSO MAFIA BOOK ONE

Nova Mason

This is a work of fiction. Names, characters, organizations, places, events, and incidents are either products of the author's imagination or are used fictitiously.

Copyright © 2022 Nova Mason
All rights reserved.

No part of this book may be reproduced, or stored in a retrieval system, or transmitted in any form or by any means, electronical, mechanical, photocopying, recording, or otherwise, without express written permission from the author.

ISBN: 8218055813
ISBN-13: 9798218055813

Cover Design: SelfPubBookCovers.com/billwyc

WARNING:

"Running" is the first book in the Caruso Mafia series. It is a stand-alone Mafia Arranged Marriage Romance, complete with HEA and no cliffhangers.

Please note: this book is a mafia romance that contains mature content, graphic violence and may contain triggers. If such materials offend you, please do not read.

CHAPTER ONE

Seven Years Ago - Luca

There is nothing quite like being summoned to the Don's private office at seven am on a Monday morning to start your week off right. Yes, that is sarcasm. It's been a rough couple of days and I just want to get on with my normal shit. I am tired and still seething from the betrayal I discovered.

On Saturday evening I got a call from the Port Master at our docks. He claimed our usual shipment of guns had been delayed. I don't like kinks or deviations in our plans. Call me controlling, but when you sit at the table of a multi-billion dollar mafia empire that was built on blood with enemies searching for ways to extract more, you crave control. Demand it even.

Not willing to accept the delay as is, I hopped into my SUV with my closest men. Massimo my best friend and trusted enforcer, Val my blood brother and rising hacker, and Al my driver and bodyguard. I'd like to say I don't need a bodyguard. I can handle business and defend myself just fine. I don't, however, have eyes in the back of my head. For that I am thankful for his presence. He has saved my life on more than one occasion. Both literally and physically preventing me from getting stabbed in the back.

Being raised by the Underboss of the Caruso Family Mafia, I was made to be cold, calculating, and above all, loyal. Those three qualities are necessary for not only survival but success in our line of work. Being cold means I don't trust easy. Trust in my world could get you killed. My lack of trust was why after hanging up the phone, I had a gut feeling something wasn't right.

Could shipments be delayed due to unforeseen circumstances that were in no way malicious? Of course. Was my gut agreeing that this was one of those times? Absolutely not.

The Port Master had been in our pocket for years. He was mid fifties, married with a couple of kids. Seemed like an okay guy, though I couldn't be bothered to learn his name. It's why I always called him Port Master.

While on our way to the docks I had Val dig into his finances. It was the first place I always looked when I got a suspicion. Money talked and to shady fucks with no honor, loyalty could be bought.

Unfortunately for him, I was right. Val had accessed a bank account in his name that had been opened two days prior. A deposit of a half a million dollars had been made. Val traced the money through some offshore accounts where it had been bounced around in an effort to hide the trail before finding out the Irish Mob had initiated the transfer.

Before we got to the docks, ten minutes after our call, and five minutes after Val found the money, the Port Master had a change of heart. It was too late to be acquitted, but I listened anyway. He was immediately remorseful and pleaded for leniency. Said he was paid to report a delay in our shipment so the Irish could arrive before our men and steal our cargo. He continued to beg for forgiveness and said that once he hung up he felt the guilt and knew he had to make it right.

Once arriving at the docks, the Port Master and I, whose name I learned was Fred, had a conversation between my fists and his face. I hit him several times even though he started apologizing and begging for mercy immediately.

Ruthless. That was what my men called me. I had no patience for traitors. Even though Fred was not a soldier he was a paid employee. That warranted loyalty that he didn't have. Fred learned the cost of his betrayal, one he wasn't done paying yet. He was still breathing. For now.

After his initial beating he gave us all the details he knew on the Irish's plan. We had about an hour before they would arrive. Which was enough time for me to gather a small army of men and have them hidden in the warehouse in strategic locations to take out the men the Irish sent.

It was a blood bath. One that resulted in no loses on our side, and complete obliteration of theirs. After my men cleaned up the scene, I reminded Fred once more what would happen if he ever betrayed the Caruso Family again. I hadn't forgiven him. Not even close. And just because he was breathing now, didn't mean he would be for long.

Walking down the hall with the Don's office door in my sights, I wondered if I was about to regret letting Fred continue to breathe. I didn't make a habit of second guessing myself, so these thoughts only added to the swirling of emotions that had no place in my head.

Would the Don question my decision to let him live? He had turned himself in before he caused any damage to our operation or cost us any money and I was confident he wouldn't make that mistake again. Besides, he'd only be breathing long enough to get a suitable replacement in at the docks. The men under my direct command were keeping a close eye on him. He wouldn't run or try to betray us further without a bullet between the eyes.

The Don has been in a mood lately. If he found my actions lacking I would be punished severely. I have yet to be punished by the Don and I don't plan on ever being so. My father, on the other hand was quick to the belt when I was growing up. As his firstborn son, I was his heir. My actions reflected on him so he saw it as his obligation to correct my wrongdoings swiftly and harshly.

In my youth, I hated his lessons. I will never admit it to him, but now I am grateful for them. Learning the harsh realties of life in the mafia early kept me vigilant and has allowed me to move up the ranks quickly even with his name and position giving me leverage above others.

Fear of the whip made me the successful man I am today, and while I do not yet have the title of Underboss, I have been admitted into the Don's inner circle and granted a place at the table. An honor only two other men currently share. My father, and the Don's Uncle Santo, his Consigliere. Otherwise known as adviser.

My father, the Underboss, Ricco Mariani has been Don Bosco Caruso's best friend for years. They make an unlikely pair. While the Don is barely thirty, my father is in his mid-forties. My father is shorter at five foot eleven with a budding beer gut, or more accurately, a whiskey gut. The Don is six foot four and built like a linebacker. Before they were friends, my father was a lowly soldier. He would have likely stayed one if he hadn't gone down the wrong alley for a delivery twelve years ago.

He had a bag full of cocaine. It was meant to be dropped inside the back door of a local strip joint. Payment had already been made and the details of the drop confirmed.

Ricco turned left into an alley a half a block too earlier. Luckily for Don Bosco that he did because he was laying on the ground with three grown men kicking everywhere their boots could reach. My dad hollered for them to stop and pulled his gun out from under his shirt. The men stopped but none of them had run off like he had thought they would. Instead they called his assumed bluff and returned to kicking the crap out of the future Don.

Ricco pulled the trigger quickly. He hit two men in the chest. The third ducked behind a dumpster before he could be hit and attempted to fire back. While Ricco kept the third man focused on him. Don Bosco was able to crawl to where his own gun had been tossed during the scuffle. Instead of going for a kill shot, he got the third in the kneecap before pistol whipping him into unconsciousness.

Four hours later, my dad and future Don had the body of the last guy hanging from meat hooks in the warehouse. His face unrecognizable and body ripped to shreds with the various tools they had used to extract information on the attacker's bosses. They learned the beating had been a planned attack to take out the future Don by the Irish.

After that day they were inseparable and my dad moved up the ranks to Capo within months. Once Bosco took over as Don from his father, he immediately promoted him to Underboss. It caused a rift in the family for several months. The Underboss was a position given to blood. Much like the Don's position it was inherited by a male son.

Don Bosco was seen as stomping on that tradition until it became common knowledge that his father's Underboss had been secretly selling skin on the side. He had been using the family's clubs as hunting grounds with his son leading the drugging and kidnapping of single women off of the dance floor.

The Caruso Family may sell drugs, run guns, own sex clubs and strip joins but human trafficking was a hard limit. The Underboss and his son were given a slow death and the rest of their family was banished to Italy where members of the old family would keep a close eye on them.

I take a deep breathe. My muscles are tense. I don't remember the last time I had a day off. There is too much going on now. I should find myself a release soon though. Perhaps I'll check on Vivid, one of our newer nightclubs tonight. Even on a Monday it should be busy which means I'll have my pick of any number of women.

Standing at the closed door to the office. I need one last moment to myself before I go in. Too bad I don't get it.

No sooner do I take my breath in than do I hear the piercing scream of an excited young girl. Milan, the Don's eight year old daughter runs down the hall and launches herself at my legs.

"Luca, did you come to play with me today?" She asks. Her bright green eyes stare up at me. Her blond hair is a mess of curls. Her mother hates her hair. Ravinia is a woman whose pride and joy is her looks. She is as vain as they come. I swear she spends half her day in front of her mirror, and hundreds of thousands of dollars on cosmetics and surgery. Which is absurd. The woman is barely thirty. There is no way she needed that much work done yet. Milan is a near identical copy of her mother, with the exception of her hair. The color is a near match to the professional dye but where Milan's is curly and unruly, Ravinia's is pin straight.

I don't have time to play today. Nor do I want to play.

Milan is a sweet girl. Most of the time. It depends on how closely her mother is watching her that day. Milan craves her mother's attention and affection and often times acts out because of it. Dealing with her tantrums and meltdowns is

6

not something I have time or patience to deal with today. It requires a gentle hand and with all the shit going on, I know I will be anything but gentle.

I take another deep breathe, school my face so my anger doesn't show. "Sorry Milan." I squat down as she releases my legs. Getting eye level with her should help ease the blow I am about to land. "I've got a lot of work to do today. Maybe another day." I keep my voice as soft as I can.

Tears start to well in her eyes. Damn. "You always say that and you never do! I just want to be friends." With that she turns and runs back down the hall. Mario, her guard is standing at the bottom of the stairs watching her. He opens his arms for her to crash into.

"Come on Cupcake, why don't we go have a tea party?" The man has the patience of a saint. He's surprisingly good with kids, particularly Milan. It's not a common trait for a man in the mafia. For him it's a huge benefit seeing as he is Milan's personal guard.

I scrub my hand down my face. I am not in the mood for this crap. It's too early and I need some coffee. Maybe I won't wait until tonight to get a girl. Maybe I'll swing by the strip club and have one of them suck me off. They are always eager to give attention to a man of the family. It's one of the reasons I normally avoid using them.

I give the door a more aggressive knock than intended. "Get in here Luca." Grunts the boss. I enter. My eyes scanning the room for threats. There aren't any. There never should be any in this room. It's more protected than the White House. Armed guards outside and on the roof, an army of German Shepherds roaming the yard, and a state of the art security system are among the layers of protection at the Don's house. Even knowing this, my training is engraved in my being. Securing a room is habit.

Two opposing walls of the office have floor to ceiling bookshelves. Scattered among the books are a few trinkets. Gifts given to him as signs of respect or thanks. Tucked in the right corner by the door I just entered are two dark brown Queen Anne chairs. Between them is an antique mahogany chess table. The ongoing game between Don Bosco and my father sits idle. To my left is a leather rolled arm sofa on which my father sits.

I walk further into the room. Keeping my back to the wall as usual. Satisfied that the room holds no immediate threats, I allow my eyes to move to the Don. He is seated behind his desk. Two large, bulletproof windows on either side of the wall behind him allow me to see part of the compound beyond. For safety reasons the Don's mansion is set on fifty acres just outside the city of Chicago. There is a ten foot wall with cameras that surrounds the land with armed guards that patrol it day and night.

"You wanted to see me Boss." I say as I lean my hip against a bookshelf. It gives me the best viewpoint of the entrances to the room. The door to my left and the windows behind the Don to my right. The Don raises his eyes from his paperwork. He puts his pen down and relaxes back into his chair. If I didn't know any better I would say he was relaxed, calm even. His eyes say different. Something is haunting him. More than the usual.

There is another knock at the door and before the Don answers Santo enters. He crosses the room without a word and takes his usual perch behind the Don. His back resting against one of the high window ledges. Arms crossed over his chest. He looks more agitated than usual today. His normally crisp all black suit is wrinkled and his tie is loosened. I wonder if whatever I have been called in for is the reason behind his appearance. A quick glance at my father's well pressed suit and emotionless expression have me mildly second guessing that thought.

"Take a seat son." Says the Don as he gestures to one of the chairs in front of his desk. Fuck. He only asks men to sit if he's got bad news. I can't show fear. The Don hates fear. I mask my face. Ensuring I show no emotion. The chair is mildly comfortable. I won't relax. Can't.

There are another few minutes of silence. I want to speak, yet I know better. This could be a test. Teachings from my childhood taught me that weak men, men who have something to hide don't like silence. I am neither. So silent I stay.

"How did the shipment at the docks go? I heard there was a problem."

"Yes Don. The Port Master had been contacted by the Irish. He accepted a bribe to report our shipment delayed. The Irish intended to intercept the package." I state the facts as I continue to detail the events. No fluff. The Don already knows what happened at the Port. It would have been reported to him by one of his Captains.

"I take it he understands the predicament he put us in." Meaning does the man know he is dead if he tries to screw us over again.

"Yes Don. I spoke with him myself." Less with words and more with fists. I give a smile to the Don as I flex my fingers. His eyes focus on my bruised knuckles. A rare smile crosses his lips. "With several more shipments coming in over the next few weeks I have allowed him to keep breathing. For the moment. He is being closely watched until I get his replacement."

"Very good. You have always done well Luca."

"Thank you Don."

"Your loyalty has been tested many times. I hear you

were even approached by the Russians." Santo tenses at the Don's statement. No one in our family likes the Russians. They are loose cannons. They took over Boston a few years ago. Not that we Italians had much territory there to begin with. Our focus is Chicago, New York, Las Vegas, Detroit, and San Francisco. The five families have each claimed a city. Chicago is Caruso territory. The heads of those families make up the Council. They make the laws that we mafia men live by.

I hadn't told the Don I was approached. It wasn't a secret but as I am approached at least once a month by rivals, I no longer feel the need to report each attempt. My allegiance is to the Caruso family. I handle those spontaneous meetings the same as I always have. With a bullet between the eyes of the messenger and his head on the doorstep of the family who provoked me.

"Yes sir. Mishkin thought he could buy my loyalty."

"How much?" Asks Santo. His arms have dropped to his side. I can see the interest in his eyes. Does he believe I can be bought? That there may be even a drop of disloyalty in me?

My blood boils at the thought. My fingers itch to grab my gun and shoot him. I am as loyal as they come. I would give my life to this family. "Does it matter? There is no price I am willing to accept from any other family for my loyalty."

The Don claps his hands as he stands. His eyes stay trained on me as he rounds his desk. "That's why I chose you Luca." Chose me? "I have never doubted your loyalty. I can see the fire in your eyes. If I asked you to shoot your father. Right here. Right now. You would do it." It's not a question.

Without flinching or hesitating I retrieve my gun from its holster, flick off the safety, and aim it at my father. "Head or chest?"

"Which would you choose?" He questions. His eyes are

10

alight with excitement. He loves pain. He lives for it. While other Dons keep their hands clean once they take the throne, Don Bosco did not.

I pray this is a test. I don't really want to shoot my father. He may have been stern and unrelenting in his punishments, but he was otherwise good to me and my family. Showed me love but taught me to fight and defend the family. "Depends on what he did. Does he deserve to suffer? If so I can do a shot to the abdomen or knee to start."

The Don laughs. A hearty laugh that shakes his belly. I'm not sure I've ever heard the noise. I'm fairly certain my father hasn't either judging by the look he is giving him.

"Put the gun away son." Don says as his chuckle fades away. "I knew you were ruthless but damn. You really would have shot your father without a second thought. Ricco remind me not to piss off your son when he takes over."

Takes over? Takes over what?

I look to my father. His face gives nothing away except he looks proud.

"What am I taking over?"

"No worries son. It won't be for a few more years. We've got time to train you before the wedding." He goes back to sitting behind his desk.

"Wedding?" Shit. Don't tell me it's what I think it is. "Who's wedding?"

Don smiles proudly at me. Then gives a nod to my dad who stands and moves to stand next to me. "Yours son."

Fuck, that's what I thought they were going to say.

"What I am about to tell you stays in this room." I nod to the Don. "Ravinia and I have been trying for another child since Milan was born. I need an heir. No number of treatments have helped. The latest round of IVF has failed. Again."

11

Manners tells me to offer my condolences, though emotion is rarely seen within these walls. It is no secret that the Don needs a son. The Council requires the Don to have a direct blood connection to the family or a new family will take control. It has only happened three times among the families in America and each time it brought chaos and war. Leaving all cities weakened to our enemies. Before I can speak the Don continues.

"With no male heir, the position will go to my daughter's husband as long as the Council approves. I'm sure you can understand the predicament that puts us in." I nod. She will need a strong husband. One with good standing within the family. Someone close to the inner circle. "I have arranged a marriage for Milan. In ten years' time, she will marry my chosen successor."

The Don smiles as he puts his hand on my shoulder and gives a squeeze. Shit.

"You my boy. You will marry Milan and become the next Don."

Fuck.

"Sir?" I can't tell him no. I've never given thought to being Don. I knew my place would be Underboss and I have worked hard to prepare for the position. Regardless, I won't turn it down. I can't. It would be the biggest insult to him and Milan to do so.

He releases my shoulder and walks to the window. "You are the closest thing I have to a son. I trust you. I trust you to lead this family and I trust you will treat Milan with respect."

"Of course sir."

"Then it's settled. The Council has already agreed. The contracts just need your signature."

Santo places three stacks of paper on the desk. A copy for the Council, one for the Don, and one for me. I pick up the pen. My hand hesitating briefly. A moment of regret washes over me. I had not thought much of marrying. When I did, I assumed it would be with a woman I had chosen for myself. One I loved or lusted over and would be a good mother to my children like my mother was to me. If Milan remains her mother's shadow I have no doubt I will neither love nor lust for her, and our children will be getting a team of nannies to raise them so as to minimize her influence over their upbringing. I will not allow my children to turn out like her. I need strong not spoiled heirs.

I am sure to keep my thoughts to myself. The Don need not know my true thoughts on his wife and daughter, though I suspect from whispered conversations between him and my father, that his views are the same as mine.

Another stab of remorse hits me as I sign the first copy. I am devout to all oaths I take. Marriage is to be for life. Forsaking all others. If I am to take the oath of marriage as seriously as I do all things in life, then once I am married the only woman in my bed will be Milan. My balls seem to shrivel at the thought. I make a promise to myself to avoid her until she turns eighteen. It's already weird enough to know that I am thirteen years her senior and held my future wife the day she was born. I shudder at the memory.

Nope. If I am to ever perform my duties as a husband, I cannot interact with her while she is still a child. We will not wed until she is eighteen and we do not require to date or have a long engagement as this is an arranged marriage.

As for my needs in the meantime, as long as I keep things respectful to the Don and not be seen with a woman on my arm in public or sire any children until that time, I am free to sow my oats.

I scrawl my name on the remaining two contracts.

"Welcome to the family son." Don pulls me into a quick

hug before releasing me. "Let's get started on your training."

Ten years.

Ten years before I am a married man. To a girl that not an hour ago ran away from me crying.

Great.

CHAPTER TWO

Present Day - Elena

The smell of bleach and antiseptic burns my nose. I hate the smell of hospitals. I also hate crowds. I'm here for mom. It's my mantra. I have to keep repeating it. Everything we have ever done has led us here. I can't afford to screw anything up. We are sitting ducks unless I play my cards right.

My mother, Violet Bianco, or Charlotte Smith as she is currently known as, is sick. Kidney failure. She needs dialysis and a new kidney. Which means we have to stay put. We never stay in one place for long. Not when events that took place before I was born have haunted my mother and me my entire life.

A hit-man.

A goddamn hit-man is hunting us. He isn't the first. He won't be the last unless my plan goes according to plan. My mother hasn't told me much. She thinks she's protecting me. I wish she would trust me to protect her back. I've been doing it anyway. For years I have taken lessons from an acquaintance of hers, Ronan. He's ex-military. Won't say which branch. Says it's classified. He lives off the grid. My mom met him her first year on the run. He was in between missions when he found her in labor in her car on the side of a deserted road. Being the stand-up guy that he is, he helped delivery me, then protected us for the first two years of my life.

I long wondered if he had fallen in love with my mother. Both deny it. He claims he's not capable of love. That, I could believe. I'm not sure I believe in it either. Too much bad shit has happened. Too many so called "friends" have turned their back on us for me to trust anyone. Ronan is the closest I have come, aside from my mother.

My mother on the other hand still believes in love. Still clings to it. My father was her high school sweetheart. She loved him with all her heart. Still does. She ran from him to protect us and him. His life was threatened. She knew the threat was real. It broke her to leave him. I'm not sure she has healed from it, even after all these years. It doesn't help that she is constantly reminded of it. Each time we run, each threat she receives is a reminder of what she once had. What she protects. She says he doesn't even know I exist.

I often wonder what would happen if he did. Would he care? Would he embrace his role as father? Does he remember my mother? Does he know of her sacrifice for him?

Shortly after my second birthday the first hit-man found us. Ronan took care of him. After that my mother knew we needed to leave. We wouldn't be safe staying in one place for long. Ronan agreed. He set us up with new identities, a car, and money.

We have kept in contact with him over the years. Since I was ten, I have spent a month with him each summer and two weeks in the winter training. My mother protested at first. Until the ninth hit-man came. He came in the dark.

Disabled the alarm system on our apartment and crept into her room. I am a light sleeper. Ronan trained my body to listen for danger even when sleeping. It was gruesome training. Two weeks in the wilderness every year alone with Ronan "hunting" me. Keeping me on my toes even in the dead of night. Never knowing when I would wake up with a spider in my blanket, or a snake wrapped around my ankles. I hate them both. I know they are ridiculous fears, but they genuinely freak me out. I have seen brains splattered on concrete and a man's intestines lying outside his body without so much as blinking. Put a spider in front of me and I lose my shit.

In addition to Ronan's training. I frequent the gym to stay in peak physical condition, and take various martial arts and self-defense classes. My body is my best weapon. My mind is second. Though my friend Luna likes to think otherwise.

Luna is a hacker. The world's best. There isn't a system she can't get into. She's been my mentor for the last three years. We came across each other on the dark web. I was searching for information on my father. She kept blocking me. I attacked back but got nowhere. Just before I was going to slam my laptop shut and give up. Her face appeared on my screen. She had hacked my computer and camera.

I remember instantly freezing. Not having any idea what to do. My first thought was that she was one of the hit-men or at least working for them. Even after she assured me she wasn't I didn't trust her. I trust her now. Or at least as much as I allow myself to trust anyone. She has spent years teaching me about computers and how to gain access to camera and security systems that otherwise would have taken me decades to learn on my own. Not to toot my own horn, but I have gotten pretty damn good.

It turned out that Luna was also looking for someone.

The man who killed her father. He was a NYC cop. Killed in the line of duty. He was a good man, a good cop. Not a bad word could be said about him. The same can't be said for his partner. Luna says he murdered her father because he learned what illegal crap he was up to and tried to get him to stop. After that, he went dark. He quit the force and went underground. Luna has been hunting him ever since. He has connections in the underworld that are protecting him.

She says she's close. She knows just where he is. I get the feeling she is taunting him. Keeping him scared and running just to mess with him. Luna doesn't deal in blood. Not like I have to. I don't want to. It comes with the territory. In my life its kill or be killed. I never kill an innocent. Only those that hunt me, and eventually those on my list. The list of people who threaten my mother and me, but also my father and his family. I hold no love for him. I could leave his threats off my list if I wanted to. I don't. Vengeance keeps my blood pumping. It fuels my adrenalin and keeps me vigilant.

I enter my mom's room. She's sleeping. I take my usual spot in the chair I've pulled close to her bed. My back to the wall. Tablet on my lap. Feet up on the bed next to hers. She's been sleeping a lot lately. I can only imagine the pain she must be in. When she's awake she tells me she is fine. It's a lie. The weight of our running and the danger of staying in one place weighs on her every day we stay here. I want to take her and run. Run as far away as I can. If only I was a match. I would have given her my Kidney in a heartbeat.

She's on the waiting list for one. I hate it. The best odds she has of getting a match is a family member. When she ran she left them behind. They think she died twenty years ago.

It's why we are here. In Chicago. My mother's hometown. It's why I'm on edge. My father is here. In this city. As is the man who put the hit out on my mother.

Us being here is twofold. One, to get my mother a Kidney and her strength back. The second, vengeance.

I'm waiting for Luna's signal. She's helping me with my plan. I'm going after the man who threatened my family. By nightfall the hit should be called off and my mother free to contact her family. We will finally be able to stop running. We can settle down. Buy a house. Put down roots. I'm not sure if I'll be able to do it. I've never known that kind of stability. For my mother though, I'll try anything.

My cell phone dings from my pocket. Before I can look I know it's a text message.

Cold feet? It's Luna.

Warm as can be. I type back.

Good. ETA twenty minutes. Move your pretty butt.

I laugh. It feels good to laugh. Maybe when this is all over I will laugh more.

CHAPTER THREE

Luca

The walk with the Don to his office is quiet. The eeriness of it sets me on edge. It's rare the house is this quiet. There are always dozens of people milling about. From soldiers, capos, maids, to gardeners. You name it and they are here. The house isn't so much a house as it is a mansion. It's the headquarters for the Caruso Family.

It's one of those old money houses. Been in the family for generations. Ever since the family came to rule the city in 1904. The house isn't my style. I prefer modern architecture. Clean lines and minimal clutter. The walls here are lined with paintings, sculptures, and various works of art. They are worth hundreds of millions. As far as I know the Don isn't an art enthusiast. He pays no mind to the artwork once it's in his possession.

I long thought he bought it for someone in the family. Now I think collecting art has become a habit for the Don. Something he can do that makes him feel powerful by shelling out millions for a canvas while being unrelated to the darker side of business.

The Don doesn't say anything as we meander down the hall. We rarely need to communicate on our walks. After working side by side the last seven years we have developed a bond. Don Caruso, my father and me. Our roles as Don, Underboss, and Heir have been blurred, but it works for us. Piece by piece the Don has been handing over more responsibilities to me and my father has begun to train my chosen second, my childhood friend Massimo. We've had each other's backs since we were in diapers.

The council approved his position this past Sunday at their monthly gathering. It needed to be approved, as the position should have gone to Val. He didn't want it. His skill set aligns with another position I want filled, and quickly. Consigliere. Santo is near age to retire and his verbal brawls with Bosco are grating on everyone's nerves.

When I take over, Val will become my adviser which will work well with his computer and sleuthing skills. The Council meeting was a reminder I didn't need. Three years. I've got three years before my wedding. Shortly after that, I will also be sworn in as Don. Bosco will stay on as a secondary adviser, as will my father.

I am looking forward to being Don. I am not looking forward to being tied to Milan. Over the years my fears have come true. She is exactly like her mother. A spoiled pain in the ass. She's fifteen years old, dresses like she's going to the club, wears heels that would make a stripper trip, and make-up so heavy that I'm surprised her cheek muscles can move.

I feel sorry for her. Her mother has manipulated her into thinking that short tight dresses, heels and makeup are what a man wants. Not me. Absolutely not me. I like natural beauty. I like a woman who is comfortable in her own skin. I suppose it doesn't matter what she looks like. We're not marrying for love. I only need to have sex with her to have an heir. The rest of the time we can have separate bedrooms. Maybe even separate wings like the Don has with Ravinia.

That woman is going to drive the Don to a stroke someday soon. To keep her out of his hair he has given her a credit card with a near endless limit. Massimo and I have agreed that she has taken it as a challenge to max it out.

The closer we get to the office the more a sense of dread washes over me. I stop and look around the hallway. Squinting to see into the shadows. I see nothing out of place. My instincts are on high alert. I know better than to ignore the feeling. There's something I'm not seeing.

"Everything alright Luca?" Asks the Don.

"Not sure Sir. I have a bad feeling."

"Quit with the sir shit. How many times I got to tell you? I ain't that old."

"Still the boss sir."

"Bosco." He reminds me with a huff. "For fucks sake. Quit being so damn formal. You'll be taking over for me before you know it." He says it with a reassuring smile. It is anything but. It is a deadline hanging over my head. Three more years to get my fill of women and sex. Other Dons and Capos choose not to be faithful. They keep mistresses. I won't be one of them. I will be like my Don. Shit. Bosco. I will be like Bosco. I won't have a mistress. I may not love my wife but I will honor my vows.

I open the door to the office. The hair on my neck instantly prickles. Someone's in here. I use one hand to pull Bosco behind me, the other goes for my gun. Before I can aim I feel a gun press against my temple.

"Drop it." Holy shit that voice is sexy. I want to look at the woman who owns it. It's deeper than the women I have spent time with. I lower my gun to the ground. "One strapped to your ankle too."

Fuck was that a good guess or did she know? Shit how did she get in here?

"You too Bosco. One on your back and the blade in your breast pocket." Holy hell she has been watching us. No one can guess those specifics and not have been watching.

I hear Bosco dropping his weapons. Assuming she is watching him and her attention is off of me, I spin to knock her gun loose. She was expecting it. It was like she knew what I was going to do before I did it. I missed the gun and she sent a right hook to my left ear while I was still swinging. Followed by a kick to my dick and a knee to my gut. Damn. I don't know whether to worship her or kick her ass. It's been so long since someone has bested me in a fight. Never a woman.

I'm still gasping for breath, one hand on my gut one covering my goods in case she tries to kick me again when I feel the press of the gun to the back of my head. "Have a seat." Her voice is calm. No hint of fatigue from giving me an ass kicking. She stays behind us. There is a click. Without looking I know it is the door. Locking us in. Normally I wouldn't be bothered. It's two against one in here and the compound is crawling with guards. Then again. The mansion should be impenetrable, yet somehow she didn't trigger an alarm and made it into the Don's personal study undetected.

Bosco moves to take the seat behind his desk. A quick tut from the woman behind us and he stops. We both turn to look at her. She is picking up our weapons. Hers is still trained on me.

Damn she is beautiful. Young. Maybe early twenties. Her brown hair is long and wavy. Not a stitch of make-up on her face. She wears skin tight jeans that hug her every curve, and a loose black V-neck long sleeve shirt. Her blue eyes hold my gaze. She doesn't look away. The men in the family avoid my eyes. I've been told that my intensity scares them. She doesn't cower. If anything she looks intrigued by me. Like she's studying me.

Look away baby, I'm all yours.

What the hell is wrong with me? I don't know her. She still has her damn gun pointed at me. Clearly she is the enemy. One we didn't know existed. I wonder which family sent her. I have heard no rumor of a female enforcer in our city.

If she was in our family, I wouldn't risk her. She is too beautiful. Too delicate looking to be doing a man's work like this. Not to say women aren't strong. They sure as hell are, some more so than men. It takes strength to raise children in this family. To send husbands and sons out onto the streets while they wait at home. Women in our family are protected, cherished. Clearly this girl's family doesn't share that sentiment. If she were mine, I'd chain her to our bed and never let her out.

My increasingly dirty thoughts are thankfully pause when Bosco speaks up. "Who are you? What is it you want?"

She smiles. She fucking smiles. It's beautiful. Brilliant white, straight teeth shine in the light of the sun. "Have a seat. We're waiting on a few more people to arrive."

Reluctantly the two of us sit. I keep my eyes trained on her. Biding my time. That's what I need to do. She'll drop her guard or make a mistake soon and when she does I can make my move. She's proved she's got training. Even so, if I can catch her off guard my muscle strength should be enough to overpower her.

Moving gracefully she flits behind the desk and takes the seat in the Don's chair. She kicks up her feet. I see and feel Bosco tense beside me. She is being intentionally disrespectful.

A knock at the door disturbs the silence. She kicks her feet down and grabs the keyboard. A few seconds pass as she taps away at the keys before she smiles again. "Good. They're here." Well that sounded ominous. Did she mean one of our men is here, the one she wants, or was she waiting for back up? I don't have to wonder long. She pushes another few buttons and the lock for the door clicks and disengages. I didn't know Bosco had that feature installed. The look on Bosco's face shows he didn't either. Fuck. How long has this woman had access to the compound?

She stands and straightens her shirt. "Come in." It sounds false and higher than she previously spoke. Like it's coated in sugar when this situation is anything but sweet.

I turn to watch as my dad and Santo walk in. She still has her gun drawn. It's pointed at Santos. The smile is gone from her face. "Ricco. Be a dear and lock the door."

Ricco looks from her to me to Bosco clearly surprised by what he has just walked into. Bosco gives a nod. He is being smart. Don't piss off the woman with the gun. Especially until we gather more information. Who is she? How did she get in here undetected? What does she want?

After the door is locked again, she beckons the two men closer. "Guns on the floor. Kick them into the corner." With a nod from Bosco they do as she asks. "Ricco. Take a seat on the couch. I know it's your favorite spot." Surprise flashes on both their faces. Then no sooner does my father step away from Santo then does her gun go off. I dive for Bosco and pull him to the ground with me. My hand goes under the end table we rolled next to. I search for the gun that we keep strapped to the underside. It's not there. "Five." Her voice is barely a whisper.

I sit up so I can assess the room. She hasn't fired again.

I'm not hit, neither is Bosco. I look to my dad next. He is fine as well. Laying on the ground is Santo. He is trying not to cry out. He may not be making noise but his face is screaming that he's in pain. Blood pours from his right knee as he tries to put pressure on it.

"What the hell was that?" I can't keep the anger from my voice. She shot an unarmed man without warning.

She looks so innocent when she looks back and me. "I found all five. Don't waste your time looking."

"Five? Five what?" I am so confused by this woman. The attraction I felt is gone. She is a psycho. I find nothing attractive about the crazy ones. I've been burned too many times. My dick and I have both learned to avoid them.

"Five guns." Answers Bosco. I hadn't expected him to be the one to answer. I knew of only three guns hidden around the room. Where the hell had the other two been? And how did she know and I didn't?

"Bingo." She taps the side of her nose then goes back to Bosco's chair. "Sorry about the blood and mess. I thought I could control my trigger finger a little longer, but that asshole had it coming. That and so much more."

"What are you talking about? What do you want?"

She ignores me for the moment. Her fingers return to the keyboard and fly across the keys. "I am here for vengeance. Plain and simple. Santo fucked with my family, so I am going to repay the favor. That bullet was just the first step."

"What the fuck are you talking about? I don't know you." Shouts Santo.

"Want to rethink that answer?"

He glares at her. What the fuck is going on? Why would she go after Santo? He is an adviser. If anything I would think she would want Bosco or myself. Santo's title may sound powerful. In a sense it is. He has the Don's ear, however no men answer to him. Not even the Council will allow his presence in meetings.

"Listen bitch. I don't know you. Shoot me if you want. You won't make it out of this house alive."

"I got in here without tripping an alarm or being seen. Even made myself a sandwich." For emphasis she picks up a sandwich I hadn't noticed on the desk and takes a bite. She throws it back down on the plate. Once again she goes back to typing something into the computer.

Bosco goes to stand. Her hand grabs the gun quicker than I can blink. "Sit. Down."

He does. "Look. Why don't you tell us what he did? Maybe I can help."

"You already did." She doesn't glance at him. Eyes locked on the screen. One hand on the gun, one hand picks up a bag from behind the desk and drops it beside the sandwich. The zipper is open so when she plops it on the desk a stack of cash bounces out.

Bosco's eyes go wide. My eyes dart to the safe on the wall. Fuck it's open. Looks like most of the files are still there, though she could have made copies. There aren't any secrets in them. We aren't dumb enough to write that crap down. Cash is gone. There was at least a few hundred thousand. "You wanted to rob me?"

"Not the term I would use, but if it makes you feel better. Sure. I robbed you."

"What term would you use?" I growl. Her games of half answering are pissing me off.

"Child support." She says it without a hint of sarcasm.

"Child support? What the hell are you talking about?"

"Ask Santo."

My father speaks first. None of us knew he had a kid. Shit, is she his kid? That's messed up that she shot him.

"Santo, you have a kid?"

"Fuck no. She's lying."

"Now, now Santo. We both know I'm not the liar. Tell him." She gets up and moves to the window. She settles herself in the same position Santo usually takes. Back against the ledge, arms across her chest. Her gun still easily available to shoot at any moment. "Tell your nephew what you did to Violet."

Bosco tenses. His eyes go wide. Why is that name familiar?

"Violet?" Bosco whispers.

"Tell him Santo. Tell Bosco how you threatened his wife to leave the city. How you held a gun to her unborn child and forced her to leave behind everyone she knew. Tell them how you faked her death."

Bosco rises. The anger in his eyes brings a chill to my skin. Shit. He threatened Ravinia?

"You threatened my wife? You threatened my Violet? Where is she?"

To Santo's credit he doesn't cower as Bosco screams and towers over him. "I got rid of that worthless bitch before she dragged you down. Before she dragged down the whole family." Bosco kicks Santo in his injured knee. He cries out.

"She was my wife. My Queen. She saved my life. She would have been a better partner than that whore I got stuck with."

"Hang on." Ricco interrupts. "Violet? Wife? You mean your high school sweetheart Violet?"

Bosco runs his fingers through his hair. The crazed and angry look in his eye hasn't diminished. "Yes. I loved her. I still love her. One weekend I took her to my father's cabin. The Irish attacked us. I was held at gunpoint while Violet hid. Or I thought she hid. The woman ignored me and snuck around them. She took both men out. Saved my life." He begins to pace behind Santo. His eyes never leaving where he lies on the floor. "I knew she was the only woman for me. That night we flew to Vegas and married in secret. Two weeks later she was gone. Santo and my father told me she had been in an accident. Her car had run off the road. It was so mangled they couldn't identify her body. They had to do a DNA test. All these years. I believed it."

I turn to the woman. "She's alive?"

"For now." She replies with absolutely no emotion.

Bosco stops pacing. "What the hell do you mean for now? If you hurt her I swear to...." He takes several aggressive steps towards her.

"You'll what?" Damn this girl has balls. "You talk a big game for a man who so quickly accepted that the woman he supposedly loved ran away. Did she seem like the type to run away when things got tough?"

His eyes soften. "No. She wasn't."

"Did you even look for her?"

"Of course I looked for her!"

"Why do I not believe that? You, with all of your resources as Don, couldn't find an eighteen year old woman, but thirty-six of your soldiers could? Thirty-six of your supposed loyal men were paid by Santo to hunt her down and put a bullet in her head."

Bosco goes back to Santo and kicks him again, and again. "You slimy piece of shit. You worthless cock-sucking asshole!"

"How do you know all this?" I ask her. For someone so young. Someone I've never seen let alone met knows more secrets of our family than the Don or myself.

"You haven't figured it out yet?" She smiles brightly. It's deceiving. There is a hellcat under that smile. A psycho not afraid to rain hell on those around her.

"You said Violet is alive. Where is she? Can I see her?" Pleads Bosco.

"Get him to call off his dogs and we'll see."

"His dogs?"

She huffs and rolls her eyes. "The contract. The hit. He has assholes still after her. Until I know she's safe from them, you aren't getting anywhere near her."

Bosco looks at Ricco. "Get the guards. I want him in the basement. Now." The basement is Bosco's personal playground. His dungeon of torture. Santo won't live through the night once the guards get him down there.

Ricco nods and goes to the door. He returns a few moments later with Massimo and Tony. While he's gone I keep my eye on the woman. She seems to know a lot, but I don't trust her. She could be lying. Violet could be dead and she is just messing with Bosco. She could be plotting to get him to second guess all those loyal to him. It could start a civil war.

Her face is calm. Her hand steady with the gun at her side. Until she lays eyes on Tony. There is an instant fire in her eye. She moves to the keyboard and slams on the keys. Bosco moves to the back of the room to talk to Massimo. Looks like he's telling him not to provoke the girl. The keys continue to slam. What the hell is she typing?

She swings the screen of the computer around. A low resolution video beings to play. Her gun goes up. It's aimed at Tony. Everyone's eyes are on the screen. I'm pretty sure I am the only one watching her. I want to move, to jump, and grab the gun but the desk is in my way. She could get off a shot before I can get to her.

A voice from the screen cuts through my thoughts. "Be a good girl. Scream loud for me. Daddy can't save you. No one is coming." I know that voice. I look to the screen. Quality is bad but there is no denying that that voice and figure on the screen is Tony. He's hovering over someone. A woman. No a girl. Too young to be tied down to the bed she is on. The image is grainy but it is obvious that she is pulling frantically at her bindings and doesn't want to be there.

Pop!

The gun goes off. A single shot. Tony falls to the floor. "Get that rapist out of my sight!" She says with a slightly raised voice. She might not be yelling but the venom of her words floods the room. Bosco grabs the gun off of Massimo and shoots Tony four more times. It wasn't necessary he was dead already. She had hit him between the eyes. A perfect kill shot.

The sounds of the girl in the video screaming pierces the air. I don't want to listen. I can only image the pain and suffering she experienced. As though the woman can read my mind she stops the video. "It gets worse. You can watch it if you need to. That asshole deserved a slower death." She sinks into the chair. Her voice dropping to almost a whisper. "I couldn't save her."

"She's dead?" She doesn't answer me with words. It looks like she is getting chocked up. She nods instead. "How many others?"

"Girls? I'm not sure." Her voices cracks before the strength in her voice returns. "At least a dozen. Three I know are dead."

Bosco hands the gun back to Massimo. I can see the confusion on his face. I would be confused too. An unknown woman is standing at the boss's desk. She shot a soldier and none of us retaliated or made a move to stop her.

"Fuck." Bosco sits on the couch. His hands pulling at his hair. I've never seen him this strung out.

"It's over now. He's dead. The girls are in counseling and getting the help they need. Besides…" She clicks another file on the computer. This time a slide show starts. "You have bigger fish to fry."

She leans back again and lets the slide play. By the third image I see what she found. Santo was meeting in secret with the Cartel. "Motherfucker." I storm over to Massimo and grab his gun. He still looks lost. I shoot Santo in the other knee. "You disloyal, backstabbing bastard."

Bosco moves to grab the gun from my hand. I know he wants to kill him. I can see it in his eyes.

"Don't kill him. Yet." She commands without looking at us. She is back to looking at the screen. We both pause and look at her. Waiting for her to continue. I still haven't figured out why neither of us are aiming Massimo's gun at her. She broke in here. She's shot two of our men. "I didn't get any audio. I have no clue what that asshole told them. Only that he was taking large deposits in an offshore account and had weekly meetings with them only hours after meeting with you all in this room."

I turn to Massimo. "Take him to the basement. I want him stripped and strapped to the chair."

"You got it." He replies as he follows my orders.

CHAPTER FOUR
Elena

"Well it's been fun catching up." I grab the bag of money, zip it shut and move to the window. I got what I came for. Bosco is going to get the hit-man called off and the rapist is dead. It's more blood on my hands but after I found out about the girls he hurt, I knew he had to die by my hand. He had to be added to my list. And I got to shoot Santo, damn did that feel good. Wish I could stay for his torture. It's a small price to pay, I need to get back to mom.

I know Bosco and Luca will continue what I started. They won't want the Cartel gaining any more traction on their territory and I just served their rat up on a silver platter.

I open the window without a sound. The men are talking, plotting. Forgetting all about me. Good. I should be able to make a quick escape. Getting in was easy. Loop all the cameras to show no movement across the compound and through the house. Turn off the alarm for thirty seconds while I picked the back door lock. Guards were easy to distract. One false alarm trigger on the south wall combined with three unexpected cabs all called to pick up a different person that doesn't exist at the gate.

Yeah my distractions worked perfectly.

During my recon and planning I had decided that trying to get the men in the room to let me out the door was an unlikely scenario once I was in. The window was a decent option. We were on the second floor so I needed to climb down or risk injury. Thankfully the building was made with large gray stones. Essentially climbing down was no more difficult than rock climbing. Until two months ago that was a skill I didn't have. That's why planning was essential to my success. Plotting my escape allowed me to practice the skill I needed to scale down the wall.

"Where do you think you are going?" A shiver runs down my back. Damn I like his deep voice. Nope. Not happening. I have never had a crush. It isn't happening now. I've been hearing his voice for years, have it memorized. Just because I like the sound of it doesn't mean I like the man that comes with it.

Though, I'm not blind. Luca is gorgeous. Tall, muscular, sharp jaw, with piercing green eyes. His hair is a lighter shade of brown then mine. Trimmed short on the sides and longer on top. It falls down his forehead almost to his eyes. Yeah if I was a normal woman I would be screwed.

My chest tightens. If only I could be normal. I'm not sure if when this is over I will be able to try. I'm too far gone. Spent too much time running. I don't make friends easy. I can't keep them worth a crap. Luna's the only one that hasn't dropped me like a hot potato.

"Leaving." I reply blandly.

"Not yet you aren't. I have some questions for you." I huff and turn to face him. I'm not surprised he has Massimo's gun pointed at me. I guess I deserve it.

34

I pull my leg back in but don't move away from the window. "You can ask. Doesn't mean I will tell you."

"Who are you? What is your name?"

I smile at him. "If you were paying attention you should having figured it out by now."

I can see my vague answers are getting to him. The anger in him is boiling up. "Enough of the games."

"Why, games are fun." He takes a step closer to me. I wonder if I could disarm him? He's got muscle. I've got speed and know all his moves. Could be an interesting fight.

"How do you know so much about us?" Asks Bosco. Crap forgot there were other people still here.

"I watched you." It's the truth. In part.

"You watched us?" It sounds like he doesn't believe me. Not like it was hard. "Why?"

"I had my reasons." It's a simple enough answer without lying.

"And they have something to do with Violet?"

"They have everything to do with her."

Bosco rounds the desk. He is only a few feet from me now. I wonder if he can see it yet. "Why? Who is she to you?"

I shake my head. Nope. Can't get caught in this web. Need to leave. "She deserves to rest. She's been running for too long. You have no idea how tiring looking over your shoulder can be."

"I'm the Don. I always have to look over my shoulder."

"It's not the same. You have people loyal to you. Friends, family, soldiers that have your back. That watch your six. And at the end of the day you have this massive house that you can lock yourself away in. Violet hasn't had that. She left everything and everyone behind to save you. No one was watching her back until I could."

"Who is she to you?" He looks like he wants to reach out

and touch me. He can probably see my resemblance to her now. I am a solid mix of the two of them. My hair is hers, same as my smile. When I smile. And I have his eyes.

I shake my head again. "Get Santo to call the dogs off of Violet." I turn to swing my leg out the window again.

"I will."

"Good."

I go to hoist the rest of my body out the window. I stop with the sound of a safety being turned off. "You aren't going anywhere."

"Damn it Luca." I mumble. Knew this asshole was going to be trouble. "What now?"

"You really expect us to let you walk out the window after all this?"

"Yes I do."

'You're delusional."

"Not the worst insult I've had. Not even top ten." I see his eyes roll.

"What's to stop me from putting a bullet in your head?"

"Bosco." I reply simply.

"You think he can protect you because you say you know Violet. How do we know you aren't lying?"

"You don't."

"So what cards do you have left to play?"

"The curiosity card." He looks puzzled. Knew that would stump him and shut his arrogant mouth. Like I hadn't thought of this scenario. Freaking amateur.

"Okay, I'll bite. What is the curiosity card?" Says Ricco.

Oh goody, someone else to join our conversation. God I hate people. I don't like crowds. They tire me, and I still have shit to do today.

"You're all curious how I got in here, what my escape plan is, will I be back, what other secrets of yours I might know, what happened to the baby Santo threaten, and where is Violet? That enough items to tide you over?"

"Baby?" Whispers Bosco.

"Yep. Did you not hear it the first time? I told you Santo held a gun to Violets unborn child the day he told her to leave."

"I heard it. Didn't believe it."

"What happened to the child?" Asks Ricco.

"Ten fingers, ten toes, born on the side of the road in the backseat of an Impala."

"Is it mine?" The hope in Bosco's eyes. God I wish to hate him in this moment. I've hated him my whole like. Now should be no different.

"Do you have to ask that question?"

"No. No I don't." He slumps down into his chair. "I have another kid. Please I need to meet them."

"No."

"No?" Snaps Luca.

"No." I reply again with more force.

"Why the hell not? It's Bosco's kid."

"One he didn't go looking for!" I yell back. My voice rising though I hadn't intended it to.

"I didn't know." Whispers Bosco. "If I had known. If I had any hope they were alive…" He trails off.

I wipe my hand down my face. I did not want to be having this conversation today. Maybe not ever. "Even if you thought they were dead. If you believed the lies you were told. Why did you not seek retribution?"

"What?" He looks perplexed.

"If someone I loved was murdered. I would burn the world to the ground." I can't hold back the venom in my voice. "You were told she was run off the road by the Cartel. Yet you didn't go after them. You must not have loved her."

"You know nothing!" Bosco screams as he jumps from his chair. "She was the love of my life."

"Was? Interesting. If she meant so much to you, you would have ran after her when she first left. You would have avenged her when you learned of her death and you would say love not loved as though she no longer holds a place in your heart even if she no longer exists." I can't help but to argue back. I have never loved anyone the way my mom does my dad. Even after all these years. "After all these years she still says she loves you. I've tried to talk her out of it, but I get my stubbornness from her."

I'm done talking now. I flip my legs out the window and drops the bag down to the ground. Luca moves closer to me. His gun pointed at my forehead.

"You really don't want to do that."

"Oh I think I do."

"Yeah well Bosco doesn't want you to. Right Bosco?" Luca keeps his gun trained on me but looks out the side of his eye to the man in question.

"Where is she?" Asks Bosco.

"Hospital."

"Why? What's wrong with her?"

"Kidney failure. It's why I came to Chicago. Call off Santo's men. Let her contact her family. Hopefully one of them is a match and willing to donate."

"Who is she to you?" He asks, though I can see he already knows the answer.

CHAPTER FIVE

Luca

"You really haven't figured it out?" Both Bosco and I give a small shake of our heads. "I'm disappointed dad. She says I have your eyes." I flip between her face and the Dons like I'm watching a tennis match.

"Dad?" Bosco gasps.

"Surprise! It was a girl." She says with absolutely no enthusiasm or affection. "You would have known if your men hadn't run your wife out of town."

Damn. I can tell she isn't going to let that go any time soon. Not that I blame her. What Santo did was shitty. Worse than shitty. It was fucked up.

"Don't go." Begs Bosco. She wasn't going to stay. You could see her itch to leave growing by the second. "What's your name? Where is Violet? Can I see her?"

"You should know my name. You picked it out."

He whispers "Elena".

"Bingo!"

"Stay. Please. I want to get to know you."

"No."

"No?" He questions as though he can't believe she would deny him while hanging out a second story window.

"I don't want a relationship with you. If not for her getting sick I never would have shown my face to you. You may have moved on, but she never did. You broke her heart and your so called family ruined her life. I won't ruin you. Not yet. So don't cross me. I have nearly twenty years of abandonment issues ready to rain hell on you. Just think of today as a tiny taste. One you don't want seconds of."

In a flash she is gone from the window and climbing down the stone wall. Bosco and I rush to the window. Massimo and Ricco are at the other one. Hidden in the bushes is a small motorcycle. She lifts the branches that she used for camouflage. Before she kick starts it there is a large boom from the far side of the compound. We can see the smoke from the window. Guards from all around run from the front gate and the house to inspect it. No doubt preparing for an attack or invasion.

None comes.

It was a diversion.

I watch as Elena drives out of the bushes. The main gate opens as she approaches and she glides past without any issue.

"What the fuck just happened?" I ask. I can't help but to shake my head at the whole morning. Santo is a traitor, Tony a rapist, the Don was married before, he has another daughter, and the daughter is a psycho.

"Do you think she was telling the truth?" My dad asks as he moves back away from the window. His eyes scan the walls and ceiling no doubt looking at the cameras like I have been. They were here for our safety, but it seems they were turned against us. We'll need to double up on our defenses. If what Elena says is true, she may not be a problem again. With the news she dropped, we can assume the Cartel will be. We need to prepare.

"Were you really married to her?" Pipes in Massimo.

Shit. That could complicate things.

"Yes." Bosco swipes his hand through his hair.

"Divorced?"

He shakes his head. "No. I believed she was dead. making me a widow and free to remarry."

"Fuck." My father says as he moves to the center of the room and begins to pace. "If you weren't divorced and Violet's not dead, your marriage to Ravinia isn't legal."

Oh shit.

"Which means Milan is my illegitimate daughter." Bosco says in response to the unasked question.

"And Elena is your rightful heir." I add.

"The council won't allow Luca to marry Milan and take over if she is my illegitimate daughter." I can't say it out loud because it would make me sound like a dick. But thank god! I did not want to marry Milan. I see the struggles Bosco goes through with Ravinia and I'd be getting her mini me.

It's been seven years since the contract was signed and I have done my best to avoid Milan like the fucking plague. She's at the age where girls start to take an interest in guys. On more than one occasion she has hunted me down. She wants me to give her a ring now. Not happening. Fifteen is too young. I can't and won't cross that bridge.

I'd like to say that is the worst of it. It's not. Her mother is just as bad. She is like a little vulture. Swooping in at every opportunity to throw Milan at me. I try my best to be polite and extract myself from their claws nicely. It doesn't always work. I've had Milan run off crying at least twice on me in the last year.

Aside from her actions, her outfits make me cringe. It's like Ravinia is trying to sex up her fifteen year old daughter so I claim her early. She wears high heels. Every day, everywhere! And the make-up, the fake nails, and tight dresses...ugh! I'm all for a woman expressing herself and feeling confident in their own skin. It's a major turn on. In Milan's case. It's a turn off. Not that I needed an off. Underage girls don't do anything for me. I don't look twice at them.

Bosco has tried to reign Milan and the mother in. It just leads to whining and headaches. The Don doesn't have time for it. We just ended a second war with the Irish, the Russians are breathing down our necks and now we have learned that the Cartel had insider information on us.

"Elena." Says Massimo to no one in particular.

Apparently I'm not the only one thinking about her. "We need to find her. We don't know what else she knows." Says Ricco. "We need to find out what she can tell us about the Cartel."

"She seemed to know an awful lot about Santo and his schemes." Adds Massimo.

Bosco is deep in thought. He hums in agreement but I'm not sure he was listening.

"Don....what are you thinking?" I have a feeling I'm not going to like what's coming next.

CHAPTER SIX

Luca

"Elena..." I start, hoping it will prompt Bosco to say what is on his mind.

"Yes. Elena, we are all thinking about that she-devil." Growls Ricco.

"That's my goddamn daughter! You treat her with respect!"

"How can you be so sure?"

Bosco turns the computer monitor that he's been staring at around. On the screen are four photos. One of the Don and Violet at what I can now assume is their wedding in Vegas. The two of them are dressed nice, but casual. There isn't much in the details to signal they just wed. There is an Elvis impersonator, but those are on every street corner in Vegas. I've seen the photo before. It didn't mean anything to me at the time. He keeps a framed copy in his desk drawer. He pulls it out and flips it around for all of us to see.

Next photo is of a Violet in a hospital bed, a newborn with dark tufts of hair and blue eyes. Another of Violet that appears to be ten years later. Beside her is a little girl. With brown hair and blue eyes. Looking an awful lot like Elena. The final photo was at what appears to be a graduation ceremony with Violet and Elena standing under a congratulations banner. In every photo there is no denying they are Violet and Elena.

Bosco goes over to his bookshelf and pulls open a photo album. The picture on the right is the one he is looking at. It is of a little boy, about ten years old. Aside from the long hair, it looks just like the girl from the second photo. "She looks just like me."

I can't help but to whisper "only prettier". Guess my whisper wasn't so quiet. The room breaks out into laughter.

"Thank god for that." Ricco seems to be on the same wavelength as Bosco. "We would need a DNA test to confirm."

"It appears she already thought of that." I say motioning to the partially eaten sandwich and glass of empty milk. Her DNA will be on both.

Bosco grabs a glass from his bar cart and pours a glass of whiskey. Chugs it back then gives both glasses to Ricco. "Take these to the boys in the lab. Have them put a rush on it."

"Yes boss."

"And call in Valentino on your way." Ricco leaves and Valentino, or better known as Val, enters. The family has been looking into improving its systems and upgrading firewalls in recent years and Val has taken it as his personal mission to lead the charge. That's where Val's skills are best suited. He's not built to be all muscle. He's on the leaner side. He never would have made a good enforcer like Dad wanted. That's why I have Massimo. He's ruthless like me all the time, while Val is ruthless when necessary. I trust him. He won't ever deceive me or the family like Santo.

After today, Val is going to need to double his efforts to upgrade our systems. If Elena could infiltrate the compound without breaking a sweat, it means someone else could too. Val is going to be very busy.

Moving quickly, not looking at anyone, Val takes his usual spot in the corner. His fingers never stopping from flying across the keyboard of his laptop that he has open and held with one hand. "Already got the system back up. No idea how the hell she got past my firewall. Apologies Don. I'll fix it." Of course he is already on it. Val hates failure. It eats away at him. More than the blood on his hands.

"Wonderful. In addition to that, we need you to find that girl and her mother. Violet Bianco and the daughter is Elena."

"On it boss."

A minute later and he says he found her. "Already?" I question. It couldn't have been that easy.

"Yes, why? Doubt me?" Val looked disappointed. He is a smart guy. Shy as hell and not entirely confident in himself. Not yet anyway. By the time I take over he will be the man I need him to be to help me lead.

"No, but she's been in hiding for twenty years. I find it strange that she covered her tracks all those years, and not now."

"Huh that is interesting. She definitely isn't hiding anymore." Val flips his laptop around so we can see. Looks like I'm looking at an inpatient form. "Her name is clearly registered at the hospital. Our hospital."

The hospital was an investment I brought to the table years ago. We needed a way to wash more money while cementing our presence in another corner of the city. As it was a private hospital, it also meant we would have full control of the staffing. More than half of them are in the family. The rest are paid generously to look the other way when needed.

Having the hospital also means we can send our injured men in through the basement to be treated when we would otherwise need to resort to shady back rooms.

Hospitals are required to report bullet wounds to the police. Except in our hospital, when it is one of our men. They are given the best treatment possible and a safe room to recover without law enforcement coming to ask questions.

Fuck. Elena must have been telling us the truth about Violet.

"What is she there for?" I sense a hint of panic in Bosco's voice.

"Dialysis. She needs a Kidney. They have her on the wait-list."

"Elena wasn't lying." Says Massimo.

"It appears not, but can we trust her?" I mull it over. Saying it out loud. Not expecting anyone to reply.

Minutes tick by. I'm no closer to my answer when Bosco speaks up. "Massimo, round up a team. I need to find my wife and daughter. We need to go after her."

"Yes we do." I say in agreement. Best to have her close so I can keep an eye on her. My gut is telling me she is going to be trouble.

"I'll get right on it." Massimo replies and turns to leave. I make to follow.

"Luca..." Bosco's voice has turned tight. It sends a shiver up my spine for the second, maybe even third time today.

"Yes Bosco?"

"Tread carefully."

"Are you sure sir?" I have to ask even though I know he is certain. If I were him and just learned I had a daughter and my wife I believed dead was alive, I'd be questioning everything too. "Even if she is your daughter, we don't know what her plans are. She wasn't raised in the family."

"No, she wasn't." He pauses to take a breath. "But she is my rightful heir." My hair stands further up if that is even possible. "A blood relative born of two married parents."

I don't like where he is going with this. "Sir...."

"Once the news gets out that my marriage to Ravinia was never legal, the family will toss out the contract for your marriage to Milan." He pauses for a split second. "Elena is my blood. I can feel it. When the DNA test confirms it, we will bring her and Violet home."

"Yes sir."

"And then you and Elena will marry."

Fuck!

"Boss? She's clearly dangerous, and out of control. Do you really want to give her more power? The families won't know if they can trust her. I don't know if I can trust her."

Bosco laughs. He freaking laughs!

"Her mother wasn't liked at first by the families either. Especially my father. She wasn't born to a family in our life. She was Italian which was the only reason my father humored my so called high school crush." He wanders over to the couch. He pats the seat next to him. "Come, I have a story I need to share."

I take my place beside him and wait in silence while he gathers his thoughts.

"My father didn't want me to date her, and the council expressed deep concern with Violet's ability to reign at my side. They said I needed someone strong. Someone who knew the inner workings of the family. Violet was naive to the family business before we started dating. After our third date, when I knew I was going to marry her someday, I began to teach her about the family.

"None of the secrets, but the stuff any kid our age who wasn't the Don's kid would know. She absorbed everything I said. She didn't complain and in fact begged me to train her to fight. I had told her my gruesome path to being a made man and the tests my father put me through. She thought it only fair that she goes through a trial as well. We hit the gym nearly every day after school and on weekends I took her to the gun range to practice." Bosco rubs at the scruff on his chin. "I already told some of this story earlier, so bear with me. At eighteen we were on a date. I had taken us away for a romantic weekend. We were at my father's cabin away from the city. A perimeter alarm went off in the night. When I didn't come back inside, Violet came out to find me. I was on my knees, a gun to my head. The two men were planning on filming my assassination and sending it to the families.

"Violet was smart, and courageous. She had learned from our time together that a day might come when one or both of us would be either attacked or kidnapped. I knew she was strong. Knew she'd make a great Queen. That day she proved she was the strongest person I ever met. Except maybe Elena. I didn't hear or see her until I felt the dropping of blood on my head and the sound of a body hitting the ground behind me." He smiled as he retold the memory. "She had slit the man's throat, pushed me aside, dove for the gun and shot the man setting up the camera before he could even look up. She saved my life. I asked her to marry me right there and then while we were covered in the blood of our enemies." He pauses again. The sadness returning to his voice. "Violet has been protecting my daughter all these years. She raised her to be strong. With what Elena showed today, I don't doubt she will be ready in a few years to take the throne with you."

"Yeah, if we don't kill each other first." I reply with a half hearted laugh. I'm serious though.

Bosco laughs at that. "I love you boy. As if you were my own son. But if you hurt her, well, you can use your imagination. Come on, let's go make a traitor bleed."

CHAPTER SEVEN

Elena

I smile as my phones rings. Name says "answer bitch". It should say "unknown number". For as good as my hacking skills are, Luna is a hundred times better. She's like a ghost. A friendly ghost. She's taught me a lot over the years. Though we have only met once in person, we talk frequently. Luna always initiates.

Not that I don't want to some days. Like I said I am shit at keeping friends. For Luna though, I'd try. I just don't have her number and every attempt I have made at tracing her has come up empty. I keep trying though.

Luna says the day I find her is the day I will have surpassed the master. Luna isn't her real name. She won't tell me it. I don't blame her. She runs from greater dangers than me. Her hunt for her father's killer has caught the attention of a man more powerful than my father. More resources too.

Luna is the name she gave herself. She says it's because like the moon, you may not always see her, but she is always there. And sometimes even when it is shining brightest, still no one pays attention to it. And when it is hidden in shadows, its effect is just as strong. Her abilities give her access to more secrets than any one being should know. Her influence over the underground world is unheard of. Literally. People can feel the strings she pulls, but no one knows they are controlled by one person. One being her.

I don't envy her. I respect her. To a small degree I trust her. As much as I can anyway.

I answer the phone, before I can greet her, Luna speaks. "How did it go?"

A laugh escapes me. "You know how it went."

"Of course I know how it went. But I still like to hear it from you." She was watching the cameras. Having my back from a distance like always.

I can't help the smile that spreads across my face. It's probably the most genuine happiness I have felt in a long time. "It went well. Got the cash. The rapist is dead, and I got to shoot my uncle."

"That a girl! And that hot guy Luca!" It's not a question. It's a statement, and it bothers me. I'm not sure why. The thought of Luna drooling over him, of having access to the cameras that allow her to look in on him at any time has me clenching my teeth. "Did you get an up close and personal look at him? I would have. I would have given that fine ass a smack too."

"Luna!"

"What, he's a hot piece of ass or weren't you paying attention? Looks like you could bounce a quarter off it." She's not wrong. His ass did look nice in his slacks. They must be tailored. I should send a gift basket to the man who made them.

What? No Elena! Focus. I berate myself. I may have accomplished my task at the mansion, but I am by no means done.

"I was a little preoccupied." I reply to Luna.

"Multi-task darling. Multi-task." We aren't on a video call. I have a feeling if we were I would be getting a finger waged at me like an old grandma.

"How old are you, sixteen or sixty?" I tease.

She gives a chuckle. Neither of us laugh easy. "Ha, ha, ha. Twenty-five thank you very much."

"And why are you looking at Luca, don't you have a man?"

"Don't I wish! No. No man." The sound of her dejection has me regretting teasing her. She isn't against crushes or finding love like I am. Being a ghost hasn't stopped her from dating. Though I doubt any of them have known her name or the real her. She hides her real self well. It's protection. Like a bullet proof vest, only its one that doesn't physically weigh you down. Only mentally.

"What about that one that was hunting you, wasn't he getting close?"

"Oh, he's still hunting." The man is a god. A body made of stone with each ridge of muscle carved to perfection. He has an easy swagger about him. Confident but not cocky. Unlike Luca. That jerk has cocky written all over him. It's like cologne for him. I doubt he even realizes it.

I saw Luna's hunter once over her shoulder. She had been video chatting with me while she sat in a cafe in Paris. She got a good kick out of it and let me share in her amusement and watched as he berated his men for losing her. Silly man. They weren't even chasing the right gender. He thought the ghost was a man. Such arrogance.

The man thought he was hunting her. Really she was leading him on a chase. One she got great joy from, all while admiring him from a distance.

"He's not even on the right continent let alone the right city." She giggles and I can't help but join. We laugh together for several minutes, before we turn back to more important matters. "Will your mom be able to talk to her family again?"

"Yeah. I've been watching them since I left. Santos only had one guy on them the last few years. Claimed he thought we died but had no confirmation. He had lost too many weak soldiers over the years, so he contracted a man outside the family." It's good it's only one. Sucks that the one is far more dangerous than any that have come after us before. Which means as long as the Don followed through with calling off the hit. We were in the clear. "I think he believed the deaths we faked a few months back." Things had been quiet since then. I had hope it would stay quiet. My training taught me to remain vigilant anyway. Getting complacent meant missing signs of danger. We couldn't afford that. Not when we were so close to freedom.

"Good. That was some of my best work." Luna replies. It was gruesome. Luna had helped us plan the fake scene. We had destroyed a motel room to look like a fight had taken place. I made sure to leave DNA all over the room and a chunk of our belongings. For weeks leading up to it, mom and I had been drawing vials of blood that we could splatter around the room. It was enough blood that without our bodies, it would look like we bled to death shortly before or after our bodies were moved. "The bloodier the better!" Says the woman who hates blood.

I shake my head. "I saw that bitch." She says with another laugh. Smiling, I look up and find the nearest camera. I flip it the bird, knowing Luna is watching me through it. "You know they are tracking you."

"I know."

"I saw two SUVs and a motorcycle."

"They've got their main Doctor on the floor today. I'm sure they've already made a call to him." It's why I chose this hospital. It's not public knowledge, but this hospital is privately owned by none other than dear old dad and the family. I have mom registered as both Violet and Charlotte. I need her information on file for the transplant, and to throw off the assassin. He either would follow me here where the room for Violet would be empty. Or he would ignore it. Thinking I was messing with him. That would be true for both ways. I needed a backup plan to draw him out safely if Bosco didn't get Santo to call off the hit.

I blackmailed one of the nurses at the front desk to check in Violet into an empty room. Meanwhile I had Charlotte in for dialysis. I had manipulated her paperwork enough to get her proper treatment without it being able to be tracked back to her true identity.

"Oh, you devious girl."

"I figured I'd save Bosco some work. He was going to find us whether I drove him here in handcuffs or he 'tracked me'." I use finger quotes directed to the camera. Like they could track me? If I wanted to hide, I could.

"Men. So arrogant."

"Agreed." I say with a nod.

By now Bosco should have interrogated and tortured Santo. His men will have run the DNA I left behind on my glass from lunch to prove I am his daughter. Val, his tech guy will undoubtedly have already tracked Violet's digital footprint to this hospital. With the Doctor on payroll I'm sure Bosco already called him to check into my mother's records and do a DNA swab for proof of her identity as well. Such an easy man to manipulate into doing exactly what I intended for him to do. How on earth had he held onto the city for this long?

54

The elevator dinged for my mother's floor. "Doctor is on route now. Just grabbed a file from the nurses' station." I love having Luna in my ear. It's a better feeling than having eyes in the back of my head and twice as effective.

"Wow. I figured he would have been in the room already. Old man is losing his touch." Luna laughs at my statement.

"I may have slowed him down a bit with the red light cams on the way." She replies. I can hear her smile.

"Damn, you have all the fun."

"Perks of being me girl, but I gave you the chance at an epic entrance. Freak the doc out. Let him know you know who he is."

She has a good point. "Hey while you're working..."

"You want to know how far behind daddy dearest is?"

"Yeah, I need to prep mom. She doesn't know I went to see him."

"How long you need?"

I mull it over. "I don't know. Twenty to thirty minutes?"

"I'll make it forty-five. Daddy and Ricco are just getting in their cars now. I'm going to fuck with them a bit before they get to you. Give them a good scare you know."

"You're going to play with the traffic lights again aren't you?" I ask though I already know the answer.

"I've got one or two other ideas too. Something I need to test run before my next adventure."

Adventures. That's what she called her targets. God I love her.

"Thank you Luna."

"Anytime Elena."

I end the call just before walking into my mother's room. The Doctor is by the bed with a nurse who is swabbing my mother's cheek. I'm guessing for the DNA test.

"Sup Doctor Patty?"

He turns around to face me. His eyes roaming over my body. I wonder what daddy dearest told him about me. "Doctor Patty?" He asks.

"Yep as in Doctor Patrizio Moro. Born 1982. Graduated with honors from John Hopkins. Married to Valentina since 2014. Two kids and another one in the oven. Congratulations by the way."

"Elena!" Whisper shouts my mother.

"What? You know I don't trust anyone, of course I ran checks on everyone in the hospital."

Doc smiles and pats my mother's hands. "I'll be back to check on you later."

Before Doc gets out of the room. I stop him. "I'd watch room 418."

"Why?" He asks.

"You'll see."

CHAPTER EIGHT
Elena

"Hi Mom." My mom gives a smile and shake of her head. She doesn't know the details but she can sense I am up to trouble.

"Elena…" I know she wants to ask questions. In due time I will answer them. Well, some of them.

I move to her bed and pull the covers back. "Not here mom. Soon." I help her stand and pivot her into the wheelchair I kept in the corner. "We need to get you back to your room."

"I don't understand this Elena. We shouldn't be using my real name. Especially not here. Not this city."

Moving quickly I wheel my mom down the hall and to the elevator. I need mom to get certain tests done under "Violet" so that we are ready when she gets a match. For safety, I have her staying in "Charlotte's" room. I have falsified enough records to avoid any connections between her identities. Being two floors and a wing apart helps to avoid overlap of nurses and doctors.

I get my mom settled quickly into her room. Her face is

pale again and she's looking tired. Her eyes close as soon as her head hits the pillow. She lets her muscles relax and I take up the task of getting her into a comfortable position.

With eyes still closed my mom asks one of the many questions I am sure are burning in her mind. "Where have you been all day?"

"I had some errands to run." I hate lying to my mother, so instead I give her thin truths.

"Do those errands include stealing money from your father again?"

She pops an eye open to watch my facial expression. I can school my emotions. I choose not to around her. "Maybe."

"Darling." She takes a deep breath. I know it pains her that I went against her wishes and found out his identity. Even more that I began to skim off his profits. I told her it's the least he could do for us considering the hell Santo put her through. "I told you. You shouldn't be messing with him. His family is dangerous."

We don't say the word Mafia. She thinks she still has some secrets. She doesn't. "I know mom."

"No you don't sweetie. You have no idea what they are capable of." Both eyes are open now and she struggles to sit up. She wants to scold me like a child.

"Mom. I love you, but you suck at hiding things." I take her hand in mine and rub circles with my thumb. "Remember how I found every Christmas and Birthday present you ever tried to hide."

"I remember." She laughs. The twinkle in her eye tells me she remembers them vividly.

"Well when you try to hide things digitally your skills are worse than that. It's like you tried to hide a car under a throw pillow."

Mom huffs and falls back against the pillow. "How much

did you find?"

I could lie. Part of me wants to lie. But I can't. I won't. "Everything." This conversation has been a long time coming. She had hints of my talents. Hints of my plans. I never shared them completely. I wanted to shield her from my vengeance. She's had enough on her plate all these years.

Eyes go wide, she perks up in her bed. "What did you do?"

"I did what I had to."

"Honey." She falls back onto the bed again.

"No mom. He needed to pay. Bosco needed to know." I see her flinch at his name. I see the longing in her eyes. The desire for me to call him dad. To accept his role in my conception even if he could never be in my life. "He needed to know about Santo. He need to know how Santo threatened you and forced you to leave. He needed to know about his connection to the Cartel, and more importantly Santo needed to bleed, to pay. You didn't."

She shakes her head at me though I know she agrees.

"I didn't kill him. I shot him, but I didn't kill him. I'm pretty sure Bosco did or will if he hasn't."

"What else Elena?" She knows me so well. Even without details she knows there was more to my plan.

"Who says there's more?" She raises a single eyebrow. A soft laugh escapes my lips. "Okay, so there's more."

"Everything Elena. I need to know everything."

"Fine." I settle into the chair beside her bed. Facing the door with a hand on the gun that's hidden in my sweatshirt pocket. I tell my mom the events of the morning. Even the part where I revealed my identity. My true identity.

CHAPTER NINE

Luca

"You forgot the part where you jumped out of the two story window, blew up my wall, and hacked into my security system." Elena stares daggers at her father. Looks like she didn't want to divulge those details to her mother. I can see why. It was reckless and dangerous of her.

I stand slightly behind Bosco in the doorway of Violet's hospital room. My father is behind me and Massimo and a few guards are spread down the hallway. Violet, or Charlotte, whichever name she is going by in this room is pale and frail looking. There is no doubt the woman is beautiful even with the illness ravaging her body.

True to the attitude I glimpsed at the house earlier, Elena barks back. "You missed the beginning." She stands but keeps her hand in her pocket. Judging by the lump there I'm guessing she is concealing her gun. "I already told her I hacked your security system, how else would I have gotten into your compound with my bike and into your kitchen to make lunch?"

Bosco shakes his head as he dares to venture further into the room. Elena looks on edge. She's already shot two people today so I decide to minimize the risk of being the third by staying back. "It's good to see you again Elena."

"Jury's out on that one Bosco." She replies. Again with no emotion.

He lifts his hands in surrender then turns his attention to Violet. A lot has changed in the near twenty years since he last saw her. She is weaker, older too, but no less beautiful. I cannot fathom the thoughts running through his head. Only hours ago he found out the love of his life that he has mourned since he was a teen is alive. "Violet…" he breathes her name like it is breathing life back into his lungs.

She eyes him nervously. Her hands gripping and twisting the sheets at her waist. "Bosco." She whispers his name. From behind I watch as Bosco's shoulders rise. I would bet money that he was smiling too.

He takes cautious steps towards her until he is at her bedside. Elena sees his fingers twitching closer to her mother's hand.

"How have you been Bosco?"

The ruthless, always stoic man I have known cracks. "Miserable." The defeat he must feel at knowing he didn't protect her is evident. Her brown eyes frown at him. "Not a day has gone by that I haven't missed you. I thought you were dead but still I wondered what our life would have been like."

"I've missed you too." Tears build in her eyes. "I wanted to tell you. I tried. I tried so many times. I'm so sorry. I didn't want to leave you. I loved you." The tears escape in a waterfall down her cheeks. Elena moves and cuddles closer to her mother.

It looks like Bosco wants to crawl into the bed, wrap his

arms around her and never leave. "I loved you too. I never stopped. Please don't be sorry. You did good sweetheart." She sobs harder at that name. He grabs her hand and kisses her knuckle. "You did the right thing. You protected our daughter. Our Elena."

He reaches out towards Elena's hand. He doesn't grab it even though it's within his reach. He keeps it a few inches away, allowing her to decide is she wants to take it. After a moment's hesitation she does. "She's everything I always imagined a daughter of ours being."

Elena snorts. Ricco outright laughs. The mom smiles at him and puts her hand up to his cheek. "I really doubt you imaged our daughter breaking and entering, shooting her uncle, or blowing up your building."

"Don't forget stealing."

"You knew about the club accounts?" Violet's eyes flicker from his face to Elena's.

"Club accounts?" He asks.

Elena drops their hands and rubs the back of her neck. "Yeah. Mom's treatments aren't cheap, and with us constantly being on the run, we couldn't exactly keep a job or insurance for long, so I had to get creative. I figured being your daughter and all I was entitled to a little bit of the revenue." Bosco laughs.

My father steps around me and inches into the room. He looks like a light bulb went off in his head. "The missing 2500 every month. That's been you?"

"Yeah, I'd say sorry, but I'm not. I kinda figured it was like taking belated child support payments."

Bosco shakes his head. "I don't give a damn about the money."

"You don't?" Elena looks shocked. I have seen few emotions on her face since meeting her, aside from rage. That one I am familiar with and do not want aimed my way.

"Hell no. Take it. Take it all. I want you two."

Violet's eyes widen at his declaration. "What!" She says.

"You heard me. I'm claiming you two. You are still my wife after all."

"What about Ravinia?" Asks Elena.

"That wretched woman won't be a problem. She's currently packing her stuff and moving out to one of our penthouse apartments. There is no love between us. Never was. Our marriage was arranged by my father before he died. I held off getting married again after I thought I lost you for as long as I could. But the families were nervous with me getting older, dad on his deathbed, and me with no heir." Elena clears her throat. "No heir I knew about." She smiles. "So I took a wife in name. As long as she had her spending account full each month she was happy. We had separate wings in the house and only slept together out of necessity to get her pregnant."

"What about your other daughter. Milan?" Asks her mother.

"She's still young. She will stay with her mother most of the time, but I was hoping you two would be open to meeting her." Elena gives an awkward cough. Almost like she choked on her spit. Her mother glares at her.

"Elena!"

"What?"

"Don't you dare."

"I didn't say anything."

"Now is not the time."

"Do you really think there is going to be a good time?" I watch them going back and forth. My mind spins with what she wants to say. What other secrets does she know, and will I ever know them all?

"No. But...."

Bosco huffs. Seems I'm not the only one irritated being left in the dark. "Can someone tell me what the hell you are whispering about?"

Her mom starts, "after I confessed to Elena who you were, she kind of made it her mission to learn everything she could about you."

"Yeah I gathered that. By the way Missy, we need to continue some conversations that were started at the house." Replies Bosco.

"Yeah I know. Don't worry I'll show you everything." Says Elena.

"Okay, back to this secret." Bosco says trying to stay on topic.

"Well, when she went digging..." Her mom is taking her time. She doesn't want to tell him either.

"Oh for fucks sake. Milan isn't your biological daughter." Barks Elena.

"What?" Says Ricco, Bosco, and I in unison.

"I'm sorry Bosco. I didn't want to blurt it out, but I don't want to lie or hide anything either."

"It can't be true." I can hear the pain in his voice.

"Feel free to run your own tests. I ran three." There is a glimmer of sorrow in her voice.

"How did you get her DNA? Never mind I don't want to know." Ricco blurts. "Do you know who the father is?" She glances from Ricco to me, to her mom than dad. Moments tick by slowly.

Annoyed with the silence, Bosco finally speaks up. "Please, if you know who it is, tell me. Please."

"Mario." She mumbles. The bad-ass take no prisoners from the office is cracking, and I am enjoying every minute of her discomfort. She looks like she'd rather be anywhere else than having this conversation. Get used to it honey. We have a lot more of these awkward conversations coming.

"Really? Mario?" I ask.

Elena laughs a bit. I like her laugh. I want to hear it louder and more often. "I mean of all the guys she could have been messing around behind my dad's back with, she picked that guy!" Ricco joins her laughing.

"I'm sorry Bosco." Offers her mom. She squeezes his hand. Bosco settles himself on the side of her bed. Their entwined hands resting on her thigh.

"Not your fault honey." She smiles at the second term of endearment he has spoken.

"We don't have to tell anyone dad." Says Elena. "No one outside of this room knows."

Bosco gives a sad shake of his head. "The families will find out eventually. Especially after I bring you both home."

"Home?" Squeaks Violet.

"Yes dear. Home. Where you have always belonged."

"I can't go." He gives her a look that says don't argue. "Darling. I'm not sitting in this hospital bed because it's comfy. I'm sick."

I eye Elena. She looks like she's trying hard to mask her face. I see a glimmer of sadness in her face at the mention of her mom's illness. My body takes an involuntary step towards her. The emotion is gone, but I feel the need to wrap her in my arms and tell her it's okay. Be sad, be mad, or be angry. Whatever she needs to feel, feel it.

A soft ding echoes around the room. I pull my phone from my pocket, as does Ricco and Bosco. It sounded like a text alert. It's not me. Doesn't look like it's Dad or Bosco's either. I look to Elena who is looking at her phone. Her brows are furrowed. Something has her riled up again.

Bosco leans in and kisses Violet's cheek. "Hopefully not

for long." She tilts her head as she continues to look at him. "I have a surprise for you."

A knock at the door has us all turning to it. Massimo gives a nod then moves aside to allow an older man and woman to step into the room. Elena's grandparents. Her mom's parents.

"Violet?" Asks her grandmother hesitantly.

Bosco gives a kiss to Violet's knuckles before moving back so she has a clear view of the door. "Mom, dad?"

"Oh sweetie, we thought you were dead," cries her mom.

Elena's phone flashes again. "Shit." She whispers and pockets the phone. "Hate to interrupt, but hi. I'm Elena, I'm your granddaughter. It's nice to meet you. I need to steal Bosco for a minute." She nods to the door. Quickly she moves to it. So do Bosco, Ricco, and I. We gather into a circle. "Did your doctor have you look into room 418?"

"No, why?"

"Fucker." She takes a breath. Pinching the bridge of her nose. "I flagged him as having possible links to the Cartel. I was right, and he's about to make a move." She pulls her phone out and presses a few buttons before pulling up an image of a hospital break-room. A man dressed as a nurse and a man wearing a hospital gown are pulling guns out of a bag.

"Son of a bitch." whispers Ricco. "How many others?"

"None, yet. They didn't know we were here. I covered mom and I's tracks."

"Not good enough. If we found you, it safe to say they did too." I let my anger simmer to the surface. I thought Elena was smarter than to get caught up with the Cartel. Especially with how she reacted with Santo's transgressions.

Her hand flies quickly and smacks me in the back of the head. Oh how I want to throttle this beautiful frustrating woman. "You found what I wanted you to find. Like the glass of milk and half eaten sandwich for DNA. The pictures of me as a kid. What about all the red lights you hit? Did you not get suspicious that none of your lights went yellow before switching?"

"That was you!" Barks Ricco. She smiles at him.

"Fine." I concede. For the moment. "You covered your tracks and it's just a coincidence that they found you now."

"No, not coincidence. I knew there was a chance that Santos had suspected we were in town. The fucker has been chasing us for twenty years. I had researched every hospital within a hundred miles. My system flagged a Cartel man at 80 percent of them."

"So how did they know it was this one? And why now?" I ask.

"Really dad, this is your future Underboss?"

"Shut up." I growl and give her a good shove with my shoulder.

"Enough flirting you two." Barks Ricco.

"We aren't flirting." We say at the same time. Ricco and Bosco exchange a look. One Elena doesn't like but doesn't have time for. If she only knew.

"Any who. The variable that changed, was you guys. The Don of the Italian family, and a pack of guards going through the front door of a hospital isn't exactly discreet. Even if you own it."

"Fuck. Why didn't you warn us?" I growl. Playfulness gone. We have work to do.

"I fucking did. Why the hell else do you think I told your Doc to watch 418?"

"That could have meant anything."

Her eyes flash daggers at me. "Well I couldn't exactly scream hey doc, Cartel in 418, go shoot him, now could I?"

CHAPTER TEN

Luca

I'm going to throttle her.

She may be my future wife, but someone is going to have to stop me from killing her first. There is no way I am putting up with her smart mouth and sarcasm for the rest of our lives. Even if she is hot as fuck.

Knives at the ready, me and three of my men creep down the hallway to intercept the Cartel men. My hand itches for my gun. We need things quiet and guns make a hell of a lot of noise.

A large number of the extended family work here. We need to protect them. To a degree it also makes it easier. There is about to be a bloodbath and we can call them in to help clean up any mess made.

Elena had stayed with her father, mother, and grandparents. To help keep the innocent safe, Elena had distracted the nursing staff by messing with the alarms on several of the patient's equipment and looped the camera feeds so security wouldn't be alerted. No one critical. All harmless fun or so she said. Bosco and her used the distraction to move her mother to a bed down the hall. One that wasn't associated with her undercover identity. They should be secure there. Several of the remaining guards are hiding in plain sight along the hall nearby.

Dad and I have split up. I am to capture or kill the two men. Before leaving, Elena showed us that they were creeping up a back stairwell. My dad was going to secure the cars and exit point. Elena's mom was stable to travel. While we worked our exit plan, Bosco was quickly getting the mansion prepped for Violet. We already had a sterile room in the basement with a few beds and equipment.

Even though we had the hospital at our disposal, having a medical room was necessary. There were certain high ranking members we still couldn't take the risk of sending them to a hospital. There were security risks. As evident by the situation we are currently in. Hospitals are hard to fortify without casualties.

The compound's room was now being turned into a surgical suite. Once we get out of here, and Elena and Violet are back at the house, Doc can work on testing Violet's family to see if any are a match. Once he finds it, he can perform the surgery immediately.

And Elena would be moved in upstairs.

Right next to my bedroom.

Fuck me.

That little vixen has no idea what is in store for her. I just pray she is as trustworthy and loyal as her father seems to think. I trust my Don, but love makes people do crazy things. Bosco loves Violet. There is no doubt he always has. It wasn't a big secret in his inner circle. He didn't keep photos of Ravinia in his office. He had one of Milan on his desk and Violet's in his drawer and in his wallet. She went with him everywhere in spirit, though most of us never knew her name. We saw her presence even when he didn't speak of her.

Elena has no bond to him aside from blood and DNA, and every reason to hate him and the family. So far her information has been true and beneficial to us. Only time will truly tell if she intends to be loyal permanently.

Creeping into the stairwell, we worked our way down. A door slams above us. I slam back against the wall to hide. My men do the same. All our weapons held up high, ready to strike if the intruder isn't a friendly. The whizzing of a bullet shot through a silencer slices through the air. I duck though I'm sure if I was the one being aimed at, I would have felt the hit by now.

A body falls from above us and slams into a railing a few levels down. I look over the railing at the body. Screw the knife. I pull out my gun. It isn't one of our men.

"You're welcome." Sings Elena from above us. I twist to look up the stairs and see her gun still smoking in her hand from the floor her mother was on. "Little bastard was hiding out as a janitor." Her eyes grow wide. "Duck!" She aims her gun right at me.

Fuck. I grunt as I dive back under the cover of the stairs. Another shot from her gun rings out. Followed closely by a third.

"Shit. I'm rusty. All clear." She says as she comes stomping down the stairs. Sliding the last few steps on the rail. "Took me two shots." She moves past me.

What has this girl gone through? She hasn't batted an eye at killing anyone. Blood and violence are my life. It is the way of the Mafia men. Not our women. We protect and cherish our women and children.

I have to remember that Elena didn't grow up in this. She

grew up on the run. Moving around constantly to outsmart the hit-men chasing after her. I'm beginning to see that she may have just as much, if not more blood on her hands than me.

That thought makes me want to take the gun from her and order her back to her mother's room so I can keep her hands from getting dirtier. The other part of me wants to push her against the wall and explore her body with my hands and tongue. I want to ravage the woman who is to be my queen.

I never saw myself as wanting the strong and independent type. I like control. Both at work and in the bedroom. For Elena I can concede some power. It could be hot having her fight for control in the bedroom. Sometimes. Not every time. She'll learn.

With some training she may also do well to reign at my side. She has some rough edges. If she lets me, I can smooth them down. I think. I never wanted to try with Milan. I was content with my plan to ignore her unless necessary to interact. With Elena. I want her. All of her. Maybe a little less crazy and fewer bullets.

Together we go down the stairs. I have to fight with her a bit to get her to stay behind me. "Really Luca? Are you that misogynistic you need the female to stay behind you?"

I swipe my hand down my face. "No. I need the fucking long lost princess to stay alive so her father doesn't kill me."

"Oh right. Sorry. New to this. I'm usually a one woman show." She replies.

I turn, grab her by the arms and push her against the wall. Her breathing hitches. Her eyes flash with warning. If I'm not careful she may shoot me. It might be worth it. I step into her space further. Letting the warmth of my body blanket hers. I drop my forehead to hers. "You need to get used to having me around."

"Yeah, no thanks." She squirms but makes no real effort to escape me.

"Not asking permission princess." I give her a quick kiss on the lips. Her eyes go wide. I release her quickly and take a step back.

Stunned into silence. I will have to remember to kiss her often in the future if this is the result. I turn and signal the men to continue down the stairs. My ears listen for the opening of doors or the sounds of distance footsteps. I hear neither as we come up on the bodies Elena dropped.

One of the soldiers behind me gags. "What the fuck!" He says with a heavy breath.

I look back at Elena. She's smiling at her handy work. "You said you missed." I say while trying to understand what she meant. I don't see how she did. The second man is missing both his eyes. Two near perfect holes where his eyes once were. What was she aiming for if that was a miss?

"I did miss." She says as she steps around the body. "I was aiming for his third eye." She pokes me in the forehead as though to bring her point home. I slap her hand away.

"Let's go little psycho." I say with a nudge to her shoulder.

"I think I'd prefer Princess Psycho." She smiles deviously at me. Devious or not. I like her looking at me like that. "Like you said. Better get used to it." I huff a laugh, so do the guards.

We make it down to the bottom of the stairs. My lead guard quickly takes out the last assailant. He was waiting to ambush us. Stupid fuck. He never stood a chance.

My phone vibrates in my pocket. "All clear." I say as I read the message sent from my father. I type back that it's clear on our end too. I give a look to Elena who is scanning the cameras on her phone. She looks up and gives me a thumbs up.

I call Bosco and let him know he can get them moving Violet.

Elena's phone rings. Shit. Do I need to take that back? I look over at her screen. Where the name of the incoming caller would be is a message that reads "8 min - incoming hot."

"Fuck!" Growls Elena as she answers the phone and begins talking quickly and jumping back and forth between English and what sounds like French.

Who is this woman? And who the hell is working for her?

CHAPTER ELEVEN

Elena

"Twice in one day. This isn't good." Luna and I are strictly business right now. No pleasantries are exchanged.

"Three SUVs. Coming from the West. I've got grid lock on all roads. They are taking alleys and driving on sidewalks." Luna pauses as I hear her rapidly typing on her keyboard. "There are six driver assist vehicles that I have been able to hack and am getting them into position to block their path. I can't be certain but I think it will buy you five to six minutes on top of the eight, well now seven." I look up at a camera in the corner. It's a habit when I speak to Luna. I know she is watching my every move as we speak. It brings me comfort though I can't see her back.

"Were moving now. Can you give us green lights to the compound?"

"I'll try to work my magic."

Knowing she's multitasking over a dozen things. I feel my back for my bag. Still there. Good. "I can take over lights in six minutes. Just need my mom in the car." I switch to speaking French without thinking. Luna and I do it from time to time. It started out as practice while she was in France and I was studying it for my high school diploma. Even though I was home schooled most of the time and no one knew nor cared what second language I took, I had to be the little rebel and not take Spanish which is a more common second language in the places we've been.

"Good. You've got your tablet turned on?"

"Of course."

"Awesome. I'll have the program open when you get in the car."

"You're the best."

"Don't I know it." Call ends.

I look to Luca. I could feel his eyes on me the entire time. He's probably wondering why I was speaking in French. Curious what I might be hiding. I'm hiding a lot. Just nothing in that conversation.

I find I like pushing his buttons. And that kiss. It may have been nothing but a meeting of lips, yet it has my blood boiling with desire. I want him. I hate to say it. This is not the time to get a crush. Besides, he and I could never work. He is my father's right hand man. He grew up in the family while I've been running from it. And will continue to run after this is all over. I needed my mom safe, and with Bosco she will be. Santo is no longer a problem. Once I take care of the Cartel, the family will be safe and I can move on. To what, I'm not sure. Maybe I'll join Luna and go on her next adventure.

We get mom and everyone into the three vehicles. We break away from each other as we speed down the road. There are guards in the front seats of all the vehicles. Their weapons out and ready to fire.

Mom and Bosco are in the first car. My grandparents and Ricco in second. Luca and I in third. Before we leave the parking lot, I have my tablet out. True to her word, Luna has my programs open and ready for me. Looking at the traffic controls first, I can see we have all green lights to the compound. It seems as though all other lights are red. It's creating a grid lock that will take hours for the city to fix. It should slow down any cars that may chase us.

As we speed through the streets. I turn every light we pass back to red. "Are you doing this?" Asks Luca.

"Yes, now shh. No talking." I give him a nudge as he tries to lean into my space.

Luca turns from me and addresses Massimo. "Tell the guards we will be coming in hot. Be ready at the gate. Castle is on high alert." Massimo nods his head and pulls out his phone to send off the message. "Call a second enforcer. I need him to pick up a few people for me."

I keep an ear to what he is saying while I continue to search the street cameras for threats. If they get through the lights or are smart enough to get motorcycles to drive on the sidewalks I need to know so I can intervene.

Luca spouts off my Aunt and Uncle's names and addresses along with a cousin's school name. "Get them back to castle. They are family. They may struggle. Tell them Violet's home. They will know what that means."

Out of nowhere a car barrels into the side of our vehicle. "Son of a bitch." My tablet flies out of my hands. "Fucking cock suckers."

"Wow, quite the potty mouth you've got on you don't you sweetheart." Luca laughs as he opens his window and shoots at the windshield of the car that hit us. It was no accident. The car is filled with Cartel men.

The bullets Luca shoots ping off the windshield without piercing it. "It's bulletproof." Clearly this needs a woman's touch. I climb over him as he leans back into the car and loads another round into his gun.

My boobs right in his face. He pauses his reload to stare at them. For shit sakes. They are just boobs. I'm sure he's seen dozens of them. Leaning out the window. I aim for their tires. The front and back driver's side pop. The doors of the car open. I see their guns pointed at us. "Drive." I yell to no one in particular. Our car takes off.

Luca must have gotten his fill of the view because he now joins me firing out the window. We each take a man down.

"Nice shot." I tell him as the head of a man explodes.

"You too." Our eyes connect. I lick my lips. I shouldn't want him. I have never been with anyone. Never had a crush either. Who am I kidding? Yes I have. Luca. I've had a crush on him since I first started surveying the family years ago. I've fought it. Knowing I can't afford any distractions. I wish my body would listen to reason now. I'm practically sitting on Luca's lap. Our faces less than an inch apart. Fuck it.

I smash my lips to his. It's not graceful. Sue me. My first kiss was a peck in the stairwell after I shot a man. Luca is hot. Why not kiss him again? Not like I got a good taste the first time.

CHAPTER TWELVE

Elena

Back at the mansion. Mom gets settled in the basement. Bosco has an infirmary set up. If I didn't know any better I would think we were still in the hospital. He hasn't left her side. One of his men had brought down an arm chair for him. It's butted up to the bed. The smile on my mom's face hasn't left. Has she ever smiled this much? No. It breaks my heart to admit it. As much as I tried to be good growing up. Stay out of trouble and help her with anything she needed, our life wasn't sunshine and rainbows. Even a simple trip to the park to let me play had her on edge.

I want to hate Bosco. Hate the family and the torment they caused her. Watching him look at her with stars in his eyes dissipates my anger quicker than I can build it. He loves her. Learning she was alive and I existed couldn't have been easy to hear. I wonder how the Council has taken the news, or if they have heard at all. I suppose it doesn't matter. The way he looks at her, I know he will fight for her this time. Not that she will run. She's done running. She's home.

The family Luca had picked up has arrived. I get hugs from each of them as they come to see my mom. They otherwise ignore me. I try not to take it personally. They don't know me. That and mom is sick. I keep to the sideline. Letting mom soak up the attention and reconnect with the family she lost.

They are strangers to me and I them. I never got to bond with them as I grew up. It doesn't help I have blood splattered on me and pieces of glass still from the broken car window stuck in my hair. Suddenly I'm self-conscious about my appearance. I should have changed before they got here.

Luca comes out of nowhere and grabs my hand. "Come on Princess. We should get the blood wiped off you." It's like he can read my mind. Before I follow I give a glance at mom. "She'll be fine." He reassures me. For the first time in a really long time, I actually believe she will be.

Luca leads me up several flights of stairs. I barely take notice of where I am walking. Instead my eyes are trained on his back and shoulders. They are broad and strong and I have the overwhelming urge to dig my nails into them. I want to feel his skin on my skin.

He turns a corner and grabs onto a door handle. I shake my head to get my focus straight. He opens the door. With a hand in the small of my back he leads me into the room. It is huge. Bigger than most of the apartments my mom and I have lived in. There is a couch, coffee table, and TV on one side, a mini kitchen to the other and a large bed against the back wall. Two doors are along the wall next to the kitchen. My guess is they go to a closet and a bathroom.

The room is masculine. It's rich in dark grays with a few accents of a cream color. It smells like Luca. Is this his room?

Hand still at my back he leads me to the door on the right. Inside is an equally large and gorgeous bathroom.

There is a tub big enough for four beneath a window. A shower with multiple shower heads both above and along the wall. The tub is screaming my name. Begging for me to submerge myself in it with a half a bottle of bubble bath.

"Take a shower, or bath, whatever you like. There are soaps near both, and more in the closet here." He says while opening a tall cabinet door. He pulls out several towels and a washcloth.

Placing them on the counter, he turns and walks out without another glance. The soft click of the door lets me know I'm alone. I move to the bathtub and turn the hot water on to let it begin to fill.

Looking down at my clothes I realize I have nothing to change into. I open the door getting ready to chase down Luca and ask for some. I halt after two steps. "Um...uh." He is standing beside the bed. Naked.

"Shit." He covers himself up quickly with a shirt he had laying on the bed.

I cover my eyes and turn towards the bathroom. My heart is racing. Damn. Why does he need to look so good? I only got a quick look but the image will forever be burned into my brain. Part of his chest and arms are covered in tattoos. I could make out the family crest on his left pectoral. He had a smattering of hair across his chest and a line leading down his eight pack to his well-endowed nether region.

"Sorry. Sorry. I didn't see anything." I hear his footsteps getting closer. I move to dive into the bathroom. A hand around my stomach stops me.

"Yes you did." He gives a chuckle. His breath brushing against my ear.

"I did. But I didn't mean to."

His arm moves to my hip. He gives it a push and I spin in his arms. "You sure? You can look again." His eyes dare me to look down. I can't see but I can feel him. He has me pressed up tight to his body. I am shorter than him. Five foot five to his six foot two. The only thing between us are my clothes. "Do it Princess."

I want to sneer at him. Argue or say something rude. I don't. Instead I feel my eyes drifting lower. My mouth watering. I may be a virgin but I can appreciate the male body. My eyes wander down his chest. My hands raise to join them. I shouldn't be touching him. I can't make myself stop. His muscles are hard and his skin shivers beneath my fingers.

I pull my hands back and look back into his eyes. He is breathing heavy. He takes a step forward. I take one back. Another step and my back is against the wall. His head dips down. My tongue darts out to lick my lips. I don't get to. His mouth is on mine. Licking my lips for me and taking my tongue into his mouth. He steps forward again. I have nowhere to go. There is no more space between us. One of his hands goes to the back of my head and tangles in my hair. The other grips my hip tightly. I might have a bruise later.

We kiss for several long minutes. I don't want to stop. He starts to pull away. Before he gets far, I fling my arms around his neck and pull him back down to me. His lips smile against mine. His hips give a thrust into me. I felt his length against my hip when he first kissed me. Now it is against my stomach. Hard and almost pulsing. It digs into me. I want to reach down and touch it. Lick it. Do all the things I know other kids my age do. I've never given a lot of thought to my lack of sexual experience. Now I am and I am completely frustrated that I don't know how to act.

Where do my hands go? Do I keep them around his neck? Should I run my fingers through his hair? His hand is now on my ass. Should I put mine on his?

"Quit thinking." He says as I let out a moan. His mouth

81

moves down my chin to my neck.

"Can't help it." His hips give another thrust before he slides one of his legs between mine. The friction of his thigh against my sex makes me moan again. He swallows it with his mouth.

"Give you something else to think about." He grasps the hem of my shirt and before I can think to stop him he has it over my head and on the floor. My bra quickly following. I immediately want to cover myself. To hide the multiple scars across my torso and back. Mementos of my run ins with the hit-men of the past. "Gorgeous." He mumbles. Completely ignoring the angry red marks as his mouth latches onto one of my nipples. They ache horribly. His teeth nibble gently before he gives a good bite that he soothes with his tongue. My other nipple isn't missing out on the action. His hand tweaks and rolls it. I give another moan. My hips rolling against his thigh. I know I am wet down there. I wonder if he can feel it through my pants.

His mouth latches onto my other nipple and gives it the same treatment. My hands go to his hair. I give a tug not sure if I want to pull him off of me or pull his mouth back up to lips. I don't get a choice. His mouth is on mine again. His hands cupping my ass and lifting me into the air.

"Are you wet for me cara mia?" I can't answer even if I wanted to. His mouth is devouring mine. I'm a moaning mess. My hips still rocking only this time it's not his thigh. It's his impressive length that I'm brushing against. He gives a moan of his own.

Suddenly my feet are back on the floor. His lips pull from mine. I try to chase them but he holds my hips back. Did I do something wrong? Why is he stopping?

He taps his finger to my nose. "Stop thinking." Then his forehead presses against mine. I wait for the kissing to resume. "I can't defile you on the first day. You deserve to be cherished." My heart warms at his words. "We need to wash you."

His hands go to the buttons on my jeans. That snaps me out of my thoughts. "What are you doing?"

"Getting you naked." He says it so seriously. Like it's a normal occurrence between us. I want to stop him. I should stop him. He kisses me into silence. The warmth of his lips. The bruising way he takes me has all thought fading. Before I know it my jeans are at my ankles and he is on bended knee lifting my legs one at a time to remove them. His face is level with my sex. Can he smell my arousal? Can he see how wet he made me?

Luca groans. The sound vibrating up my legs as pulls my panties down. His fingers barely grazing my lower lips. I want him to touch me again. To spread me apart and devour me. When the hell did I become this sex crazed? Wasn't it just this morning I wanted to shoot this man?

Big calloused hands run up my legs. My skin pebbles. Wet, soft lips press below my navel. I close my eyes. Silently begging for those lips to go lower. They don't. "Soon cara mia. Soon we can explore each other's bodies. Today I just want to bathe you."

I swallow a whimper as he sweeps me into his arms and carries me into the bath. The water is near full and he shuts it off after he gets us settled into the water. My back is to his chest.

Until today I had never seen a naked man, let alone touched one. I had never been kissed and now I am in the biggest bathroom I have ever seen, naked and in the arms of an also naked man whose mouth has ravaged mine repeatedly.

His hard length is pressed against my ass. I give a wiggle.

Loving how he reacts to me. Luca gives a playful bite to my ear.

There is no more kissing while his expert hands wash me from tip to toe. I had hoped his hand would linger between my legs. I even tried provoking him by giving another wiggle against him.

He even washed my hair. Forcing a moan from me as he massaged my scalp. I had to hold back further moans. His hands felt too good.

Before I know it, we are both clean and wrapped in warm towels. He kisses me on the nose and leads me out into the bedroom. The room I now am certain is his. He lets go of my hands and walks into the closet while I stare at the bed. My body was craving to go further while I was in his arms and his lips were on me. Looking at the bed now is like being dosed with a bucket of cold water. I can't believe I was basically humping his leg and begging to be fucked. That's not who I am. I have too much planned to get distracted by a man now. Not when I am so close to having vengeance on all those that have hurt my mom and me.

Luca returns from the closet. He's wearing a pair of black slacks and a button up shirt still open so I can see his chest. In his hands are clothes. Looks like a pair of boxers and a t-shirt. "Tomorrow I'll have some clothes delivered. For now you can wear mine."

I can't look him in the eye. Shame is quickly building as I grab the clothes from him. I turn to go back into the bathroom where I can change without feeling his eyes roam over my body.

Before I can make my escape his arms are around me. Boxing me in. "What's the matter?"

"Nothing." I lie as I try to extract myself from him.

"You sure sweetheart?" He says as he nuzzles his nose

along my neck then jaw. My knees begin to buckle but he holds me steady.

I have found guys attractive in the past, though not in the way I do Luca. I had tried not to fall for his looks while I observed my dad. It was hard. Not only does he have an insanely attractive body with muscles that make me drool, he's also genuinely a good guy. I observed him interacting with staff as though they are friends. He spoke with the soldiers with authority yet when he spotted one that seemed down or off he pulled them aside and spoke to them. They always left the conversation looking lighter.

Then there is his loyalty. I have seen him tested time and time again. He does not waver. It's a rare quality. At least in my experience.

Nope. Nope. Can't let this go on. I won't be a one night stand. And there is no way he is looking for more. We barely know each other. Granted my spying has me at the advantage. It doesn't matter. I can't veer off course now.

I try again to push him away. He doesn't let me. Instead he presses his lips to mine. I try not to respond. I pinch my lips together. His teeth nip at them. His hands grasp my ass and pull me closer. Not that I had much room to go. We were already touching. Now we were smashed together. Giving up, I open my mouth and allow him to consume me. Our tongues battle for dominance. There is no real fight. I'm far less experience than him.

He pulls back with a grin. "Princess, are you a virgin?"

My eyes go wide. How the hell did he guess that? Luca gives a little laugh and grabs onto my hips and plants one last chaste kiss on my lips. I'm finally able to push him away. "You don't have to be a dick about it."

My pride is hurt. I'm not sure why. It's not like being a virgin is a bad thing. Some guys would even like that I'm untouched for them. I don't know how Luca feels about it. I shouldn't care. Yet I do.

"I'm sorry. I wasn't trying to. I was just surprised is all. The way you were staring at my bed made it pretty obvious. You looked like it was going to reach out and grab you so I could chain you to it."

"Look it's not because guys weren't interested. They were. Lots of them." I'm lying. No one was interested. I didn't let anyone close. I huff out a deep breath as I continue to explain. "Being on the run with a sick mom doesn't really leave time for dating."

Luca must have decided to take pity on me. His eyes show the sympathy I've always run from. I hate it. I move to the bathroom and aim to slam the door shut. His foot stops it. I look up at his eyes. My blood is boiling with anger. Doesn't he get that I want to be alone?

"Don't be ashamed sweetheart. I like that I'll be the only one to be inside you." He kisses my cheek and closes the door. I stand there staring at the wood.

What the hell does that mean?

CHAPTER THIRTEEN
Luca

It takes Elena an hour to leave my room. Not that I'm complaining. I want her there. Her father had assigned the room across from mine to be hers. I had other plans. If we were to be married in the future, we needed to spend time together. It didn't hurt that she was attractive as hell.

I hadn't meant to kiss and grope her like I did. The plan was to take things slow. Let her get used to my presence, maybe even become friends before I drop the marriage bomb on her. Now I am determined to have her body, but I need to keep myself in check a little longer. She isn't like the women that I take home from the bar. I don't plan to use her and walk away.

Still, sooner rather than later, she will be under me and I will be able to hear her moaning my name. The sounds she let out while I was ravaging her earlier had me hard as steel.

Little did my vixen know, she would be spending all her nights in my bed. I wouldn't initiate sex. Yet. If she made the moves first, I'd give her my body. More importantly I wanted her to crave my presence, my touch, my strength. She has been on her own for too long. I needed to break down her walls if we were to have any semblance of a relationship beyond the physical.

I could already tell our chemistry in bed would be beyond anything I had experienced. And I had a lot of experience.

Had I known I was going to be hitched to Elena from the start, I might have backed off a bit. For the last seven years I thought my wagon was chained to Milan. A girl who was only fifteen and who I had watched grow up. Hell, I held her when she was in diapers. No way would I be able to think of her as more than a little kid. I had often wondered how I would be able to consummate our marriage or give her children.

That fear was not present with Elena. She was hot as sin and I had no qualms about taking her in every position I know and then buying a book to learn more.

Years ago I gave up on the idea of loving my wife. I forced myself to get over wanting a true partnership in the home. My parents had it, and growing up it's what I thought I would have too. Being a mafia man wasn't easy. It was late nights, crazy schedules, blood, bullets, and secrets. I had longed to find someone who would soothe my broken soul when I came home. Where I could get lost in her body and her heart and forget the stress of the family. Where I could wash the mental blood splatter away.

I would never have had that with Milan. While I awaited our impending nuptials I found solace in the beds of countless women. I didn't love any of them. Shit, I don't even remember most of their names. They gave me the small reprieve I needed. For the hours I was in their bed I could forget my responsibilities. Then I'd roll over, get dresses and go back to my lonely apartment.

I had my room at the compound, but I could never bring myself to go there after a night out. Even though I wasn't yet married, it still felt wrong to sleep under the same roof as Milan after having been with someone else.

The future I was once denied is within reach again. I shouldn't be this excited. Elena has no idea. She doesn't know she will be my wife someday. She isn't going to be comfortable being a house wife like Milan. She is going to want to be in on the action. We don't typically let our woman into the fold.

Elena is going to be different. She was raised different. Raised to fight, to question, to dig, and to dole out punishment. She hasn't flinched at the sound of a gun going off, or shuttered at the sight of a mangled body. Fuck, she has caused more of the blood and chaos than any of my men this week. And she looked sexy as hell doing it. Having her straddling me while she shot at the Cartel had me hard and wanting to take her in the back seat of the car.

Shaking my head I try to remove the vision of a naked Elena. We are in a meeting. I need to focus. She is recapping to Bosco, Ricco, Massimo, Val, and myself all that she had learned about us over the years.

It was a lot. Her attention to detail was astounding. The secrets she knew were scary. With each new detail I grew more and more proud of her, as well as relieved that she was batting for our team. She may not have grown up in the family but she taught herself well. Perhaps better than Bosco would have. He would have coddled her. Bosco may be ruthless in front of his men, but he was a teddy bear to Milan, and now Elena. I suspect Violet would have pushed her hard knowing how much she wanted to please Bosco and be able to stand by his side before she was run from town.

Elena has a plethora of knowledge on the Cartel. From shipping records, to who is on their payroll with the police. They even have a Senator in the south working for them to help with red tape over the border. She has ledgers hacked from various lieutenants of upcoming shipments and drops.

The best part is the SUV Bluetooth she has access to. She says she spent time hacking as many of the Cartel's electronics as she could. Most of them belonged to low level street thugs. The local Cartel Captain's Escalade ended up being a treasure trove of knowledge. With her tablet she can click a few buttons and moments later hear the men in the car as though they were in the room with us.

"I'm still working on getting on his computer. He doesn't connect it to the network often so it's taking longer than it should. I've got back door access to his security system and Wi-Fi so it's only a matter of time before I get into it." She states all her work as though it is no big deal. It is a big deal. It's huge.

"You're in their security system?" Asks Val. He bounces up from his chair and rounds on Elena. Her smile is bright as she turns the tablet so he can see. Sitting next to her I knew what she was now showing him. She had accessed their compound's cameras. The screen was scrolling through the various feeds.

"Yep. Here, let me show you..." Elena trailed off into technical jargon that I couldn't hope to understand. Val nodded along. Hanging on her every word like it was gospel. To him, I suppose it was. It was rare that someone outmatched his skill level.

While they spoke and worked together. The rest of us moved on to creating a plan of attack. With everything Elena had learned in addition to the details that Santo squealed in the basement. We are finally in a position to take them out. If we do things right we can wipe them out of our city. Hell we might be able to wipe them out of all our cities.

Bosco agreed to share the news we found with the Council. It would gain Elena favor as his rightful heir and prove she deserved to be here, not just by blood. Her heart and dedication would win over the family. Hell, she already had the men in this room and across the compound ready to kiss the ground she walked on.

"With those plans settled, there is one more item we need to discuss." My dad and I exchange a glance. The Don has something up his sleeve. "It has already been approved by Council."

"What is it?" Asks Ricco.

"It's time we move ahead with the next generation taking over. I know our original plan was to wait another three years." He means when Milan would have been eighteen and the two of us married. "With Violet home, the mess Santo created, and this business with the Cartel, the Council and I want to expedite things. The Council wants stability. A stability I can no longer provide." I have no idea what he means. Bosco is Don. He is still young and healthy. How is he seen as unstable? As my mind races, he continues. "The Council believes a shake up of leadership is needed. And I agree." He pauses and looks over to Elena who isn't paying us a lick of attention. "I have the love of my life back. A daughter I didn't know I had. I already lost twenty years with them. I don't want to miss any more. As soon as things are settled I will be passing the mantle onto Luca. In months not years."

"Months!" I choke on the words. Shit.

Bosco continues as though I hadn't spoke. "Ricco, I want to move you to Consigliere. Val can work with you and take over when he is ready. Luca and I already turn to you for advice and you have never led us wrong. Then the Underboss position will be free for Massimo to take over." He nods to Massimo. "He's ready."

Massimo nods. "Thanks Boss."

My dad doesn't hesitate to voice his acceptance as well.

I do. I flick a look over to Elena. Her head is down and her focus completely on her task. She doesn't understand the implications of what Bosco is saying. She doesn't understand that a wedding needs to take place in order for this to happen.

This is what I have worked for. It's what I have been raised to do. I shouldn't be hesitating. There is a pull in my chest. It wants me to get Elena to join in the moment. Her place isn't yet by my side so I hesitate.

Tearing my gaze away I nod. "I would be honored."

"Great!" Bosco claps his hands and smiles. The cold-hearted boss of our world has had his heart thawed. He never used to smile. Not like this. It's a good look on him. Some may believe that he is changing, growing weak. That would be a lie. If anything he is stronger, more resolved to be hard. Violet is back and he has a new daughter to protect. You can see the determination in his eyes. He won't lose them again.

"Elena, can you join us?"

"One second." She still hasn't looked up.

Bosco locks eyes with me and gives a wink. Shit. "Now?" I whisper to him.

He gives a nod. It's discreet as Elena walks over and takes a seat next to me. I pull her close and grab her hand under the table. She doesn't pull away. Not yet. I don't doubt in a moment she will though.

"Elena, I have great news." She doesn't answer him with words. Her eyes encourage him to continue. "I am retiring."

"Congratulations?" Her voice is laced with confusion. I

think she knows there is no such thing as retirement in our world. Bosco will be stepping back, but he will no way be done with the Mafia.

"And in a few weeks, after the wedding, Luca will be taking over as Don."

She smiles brightly at me. Her eyes shining with happiness for me. I want to kiss her. Pull her in my arms and thank her while holding her so she doesn't crumble with the next bit of news. "Congrats!" There isn't confusion this time. She is genuinely happy for me. Which makes me feel worse.

"As for you my dear daughter, we must start your training right away."

Her eyebrows furrow. The happiness slowly fading. "Training?"

"Yes. You are my daughter. My first born. Heir to our family."

"You want me to be Don? You just said Luca was going to be taking over." She asks skeptically. I see the laughter begging to be released from Bosco and my father. They know the truth. The old world truth that no female will ever be Don. She can be Queen. Maybe even someday we may have a female Underboss. Never Don.

I keep her hand in mine and rub comforting circles while the Don explains why even though Elena was blood and the position was passed down through his family, as a female she couldn't be Don. She nodded along. Her face didn't give away her emotions.

This morning I would have bet she wanted to be Don. Was even making a play for it. In the little I have learned over the last sixteen hours. I know that is not the case. She doesn't want power. She wants the right people in power. What she desires is freedom and safety. Only one of which I can give her. Safety. Her freedom will be linked to me, to the family.

To a degree she will be free, but not in the ways I know she wants.

"Luca is taking over. He will be Don." He replies.

Elena nods, still looking confused. "That's good. He's been in the family the longest. The men trust him." My chest puffs at her approval. It feels good to know she believes in me.

"Good glad you agreed." Says Bosco.

"So, if not Don, what am I training for? I still want to help. I may not have been raised by you but I am your daughter. I'm part of the family."

Pride beams from Bosco. You can feel it filling the room. "Yes, you are."

"So I can help?" She looks excited.

"Absolutely." Says Bosco.

"Great. Where can I start?"

"You will need to pick out a dress."

She glances from her father to me, and back. "Huh?"

"A wedding dress to be precise." Her back stiffens. The heat of her rage is pouring off her. "We can wait until your mother is healed so she can go with you, or I can have a stylist bring the dresses here."

She tries to stand and yank her hand away. I don't let her. I pull her into my lap and whisper soothing words into her ear. She calms mildly. "Why in the hell would I need a wedding dress?" She tries to stand again. I snake my arm around her waist and won't let go. Bosco looks to me then to her. Her eyes move to Ricco who's also looking at me. She turns slowly in my lap.

"Before you freak out...." I start to say.

"Oh hell no!" She launches out of my lap. I had no hope of hanging on. She's like a wild animal that has finally been caged. She's rabid and I'm thankful that the clothes I gave her left no place to hide a weapon. We never replaced the five guns in this room either. If we had, I have no doubt she wouldn't be reaching for one. "Over my dead body!" She backs herself into a corner. Tears pool in her eyes as she looks to Bosco. "Dad you can't be serious."

"Without a blood male, I needed an alternative."

"And you have one. You already agreed and promoted him. Luca is going to be Don. So why the hell do you need me to marry him?"

"Luca has only been approved on the condition he is tied to the Caruso name by marriage. Your marriage."

"What, why? That's stupid."

"Like I said the position has to go to someone within our family. If not, the Council can entertain bids for a takeover. In the past this has led to civil war and blood in the streets. We can avoid that. With you being my daughter, once you get married that man is family, and the assumed Don."

"So I won't marry. There that settles it. If I have no husband to stake the claim, it can go to Luca. You retire like you want. Luca gets to be Don." She is scrambling for an out. I try not to take it offensively.

Bosco tries to get closer to her. She retreats. Her back slams against the bookshelf. I stand. Making my approach from an angle and slower than Bosco's. "That's not how it works. Without a definitive Don, one attached to our bloodline, the families will go to war. Each would be coming after you to force you into a marriage or end our bloodline with your death. I won't let that happen to you."

"What if I didn't exist? Very few people know about me. I can hack the records, erase all trace of my existence. The Don's unknown child could have died in infancy for all they know."

"It wouldn't matter. The family would still go to war."

Bosco genuinely looks heartbroken that he is forcing his daughter's hand. He only met her this morning and already he is giving her away.

She looks at me as the tears begin to fall. "I'm sorry Luca. You seem great and you're hot, but I have been running my entire life. I only just found my dad, and my mom is reuniting with her family. This is too much." I rush the last few steps to her. I place a hand on her cheek and tilt her head up to look at me. I want to comfort her. Aside from a hug and soothing words I am at a loss. I haven't dated. I've fucked. I'm not used to handling emotions like this. I deal with soldiers. As attractive as she is, she is still a virtual stranger.

"Dad, Bosco, could you give us a minute?" Massimo and Val have already left the room.

"Sure thing kid." Dad says.

Bosco steps closer. He opens his mouth to say something, but closes it. Pats Elena's hand and then says. "For what it's worth. I am sorry. If I could have held it off, I would have. The Council's decision is final." She doesn't say anything to him as he turns and exits. The door clicks and she falls to the ground sobbing. Shit. She has done wild and crazy shit all day. Had guns aimed at her, shot a few people, was in a car accident, met her father, and nothing not a tear or breakdown. Tell her she needs to marry and shit hits the fan.

I want to laugh at the irony that the marriage is to me when we were naked in the bath only hours ago. Not only that, just this morning I thought I was still betrothed to a fifteen year old.

Fuck was that just this morning? It's after midnight so I guess it's now yesterday morning.

"We don't need to rush this Elena. We can take this as slow as you need."

"Really? Because my dad told me to pick out a dress.

Sounds like the wedding is already planned." She sniffs back the tears. "Wait. Was it already planned? Did you know about this? Is this why you were so eager to see me naked? You wanted to know what you were getting? Wanted to sample the merchandise?" She jumps up and practically runs across the room to get away from me. The caged animal look is back.

"Elena. Stop. You're over-thinking this."

"So you didn't know?" I can't lie to her. My silence confirms her suspicions. "Oh my god. I thought you….That we…." Her breathing becomes erratic. Her hand flies to her chest. Her knees buckle as I rush to her side. She's having a panic attack. I take her in my arms. I stroke her hair with one hand and rub soothing circles on her back with the other.

"Please listen. Yes, I did know your father wanted us to marry. No, I didn't come on to you upstairs to sample the goods. I find you attractive. Your tight body gets me hard, but it's your passion, and your drive that got me hooked on you."

"You like me? And please be honest." She looks scared to ask. Like she can't believe someone could like her.

I take her chin in my hand and move her head so I can kiss her lips. "Yes Elena. I like you very much. If we weren't engaged I would date you." She barks out a laugh and snuggles into my chest. "This wasn't the way I wanted to tell you."

"You're really okay with marrying me? You don't even know me."

"You are the far better choice than my last."

"Last?" Her head perks up at me again.

I kiss her nose. "Yes, last. Seven years ago Bosco found out he couldn't have more children. My father is his best friend and Underboss. I was raised with Bosco like an Uncle

97

to me, even though he's only nine years older. At that time he asked the council to approve me to replace him as Don. In exchange I would marry his daughter Milan."

"Oh my god. I'm a home wrecker!" Her eyes start to well with tears again and she moves to bury her face. I don't let her.

"No, you're not. I don't think of Milan that way. She's was eight when I signed the contract. Fifteen now, and I have no love for her. No attraction either. I signed the contract for the family. Milan and I have no relationship. Hell, most of the time I avoid her and her mother. I would have done my duty and married her if I needed to. Lucky for me. You held a gun to my head and gave me a better choice."

"I did do that." She laughs.

"We don't know each other. We are attracted to each other and so far we have worked alongside each other well too. I think we can do that with our marriage."

"Would it be a real marriage?" She doesn't meet my eye. Her voice is low. Like a whisper.

"You mean would we have sex?" She blushes at his question and ducks her head. It's funny how the woman in my arms can be a bad-ass take no prisoners vixen one moment, and a shy timid angel the next. "Yes, Elena we would. That physical piece can wait until you are ready. I won't rush you. I won't cheat on you either. Not now, not ever. I take my vows seriously and as of this moment you are my fiancé."

"Aren't you going to ask?"

"Nope." I kiss her on the nose again. "I'm not giving you a choice. I started to fall for you the moment you kicked my ass in this very room. I'm not letting you get away." She nods but I can see the wheels turning in her head. "No more running. If you do. I will chase you. And I won't stop until you are underneath me, in bed, and I'm pounding into you and showing you how much I care for you."

I didn't think it was possible but she blushes harder. Even lets out a little snort. I pull her close and kiss her atop the head.

"The wedding will need to happen soon. We will need to be publicly presented to the families as a couple and exchange vows and rings but that's it. In private we will take things slow. We get to know each other."

"You want to get married then date me?"

I laugh. "Yeah I guess you could say that."

"What if we have nothing in common? What if we don't get along? What if after spending time together we realize we hate each other? We'll still be married. We'll be stuck together." She's panicking again.

I grab her hips and lift her so she is straddling my lap. I press her close so she can feel my erection. "Shh....Elena stop over thinking it. I already like you. You are smart and feisty. Albeit a bit psycho." She playfully hits me in the gut. "And you are also beautiful and loyal. Physically I find you very attractive." I rub her again against my hard cock. "I can already tell intimacy won't be a problem for us." She lets out a small moan as her hips begin to move on their own.

"Luca." She whispers as I stop her from moving her hips. If I let her continue I will strip her naked and take her here and now. I press my forehead to hers.

"You know basically everything there is to know about everyone in this family. So I'm guessing that means you dug things up on me too." She doesn't answer but gives me a sheepish look. "And?" I ask.

"And what?"

"Did you find any red flags? Anything to show that I'm not someone you could grow to be friends with or build a companionship with, maybe even love."

"Love?" She looks almost more taken aback by the thought of love than of marrying me.

"I know it's not often that it happens with arranged marriages, but Elena, I am serious about giving us a shot. I will be loyal to you. In every way. I want to get to know you. Find out all your quirks. You already know I have a lot." She laughs softly.

"You leave your clothes all over the floor."

"Have you been spying on me in the bedroom?" I tease.

She hesitates before saying. "Maybe...."

"You little perv." I gives her ribs a tickle. "As your fiancé I will forgive you."

"You really want to do this? If you only want to because you need to be married to be Don and avoid a war please tell me. I haven't been able to trust many people in my life and it will crush me to put my trust in this and have you break me later. I'd rather rip the blindfold off now and you tell me so I can guard myself."

The look of fear and terror in her eyes rips at my heart. "Elena." I grab her face and press my lips to her hers. "I'm all in baby. I want to be Don. I want it with you as my Queen. You got me."

"Yeah I got you."

"Good."

"So that's it? We're engaged?"

"Yeah Princess. We are."

CHAPTER FOURTEEN

Luca

Elena spends the next few nights in the basement. She wanted to be close to her mom and bond with her family. I had hoped she would spend the night with me. I knew it was too early. Like we said in the study. We need to get to know one another. We wouldn't have had sex. We might have fooled around a bit. My fiancé is hot. Even with sex off the table and her being a timid virgin, I would have wrapped my body around hers for the night as we talked. I want her to get used to my presence. My touch. She has spent too much of her life alone. Her walls of self-preservation are thick and high. I have my work cut out for me if I want her to come to me willingly.

I was never much of a cuddler. I never brought women to my bed. It was always either their place or a hotel. This way I could make my escape as soon as the sex was done. I tried not to be an asshole about it. I'm sure many of them thought I was anyway. Staying the night would have given them the wrong impression. Better to leave before they fell asleep and woke up disappointed.

My relationship with Elena would be different. It already was. I would take her feelings into account. Make sure she was satisfied before finding my own release. Then there would be no leaving the bed. Not for either of us. I was looking forward to waking up with her in my arms and finding out what it was like to have morning sex.

Until then I would take things slow. I was used to sex often and with lots of woman. For Milan it would have been hard to end seeing as I didn't hold any desire for her. With Elena it was over before she leapt out the window and drove away on her motorcycle. There will never be another woman in my life. She is it for me. And I will make damn sure I am the only man in hers.

Elena was like a hurricane storming into my life and kicking shit up everywhere. She is an enigma. One I want to learn everything I can about. I have Val looking into her past. She has hid it well. I doubt Val will be able to find much. I am at a disadvantage and am grasping at straws. Elena is strong and independent. She has reluctantly agreed to marry me. I need to find a way to ensure she doesn't run before I can tie her to me. Marriage won't be enough. I need to brand her womb. Implant my seed. Impregnate her with my child. It didn't stop Violet from running so it may not stop Elena. Difference is. I won't give up. I will hunt to the ends of the earth for her.

Bosco was led to believe Violet died. If Elena dies, I will burn the world down. No enemy of ours will be safe.

They better pray nothing happens to her. I feel the darkness in me creeping forward. The dominant side of me taking over. I don't want to scare Elena. There will be time to experiment with my dominant side in the bedroom later. For now, I need to keep it hidden from her. She's a stray that at any moment could bolt. I wonder if I should plant a tracker on her. No. The vixen would find it, and remove it.

Unless I implanted it in her. I would need to drug her. Put it in her somewhere she can't feel it. Maybe in an ass cheek. That way when I was taking her from behind I could discretely feel it below my hand. My cock stirs at the thought.

Down boy. Not yet.

Shaking my head I wipe that thought away. If Elena found out she would shoot me. Of that I have no doubt. I need to gain her trust not ruin it before I have it.

I need to focus on something else. Anything else. My cock is hard and rubbing uncomfortable against my zipper. I've already rubbed one out tonight. I'm not doing it again. I feel like a horny teenager and I hate it.

Plans. Our plans to fix the damage Santo has done to our operation. That should help get my mind off of Elena's body and all the dirty things I'm going to soon do to it.

The Intel Elena provided on the Cartel was proving not only truthful but incredibly helpful. Last night we were able to intercept a massive weapons shipment into the city. Less guns on the street for the enemy and replenishments for our own stock. This has earned Elena even more approval from the Council. I may have doubted her when she first broke in, but she is quickly proving me wrong.

She doesn't trust easily. You can see it in her eyes. Her hesitation to share too many details, yet she shared what she knew about the shipments. She wants the upper hand at all times. It's smart. It's exactly what every man in the mafia is trained to do. And she does it instinctively. The thought makes my blood boil with rage at Santo. I want to bring him back from the dead so I can kill him again.

Elena hasn't shared the full story of what she has been through. The little she has told us no doubt only scratches the surface.

Someday I'll get her to tell me everything. I'll get her to share the list of vengeance she has. Together we will cross every name off. I feel a smile stretch across my lips just thinking about the fight we will have. She will want to finish it on her own. I won't let her. She'll have to get used to it. As her husband she will have no secrets from me. Her enemies will be mine.

Yelling from downstairs brings me out of my thoughts. Sounds like Ravinia's home. I creep out of my room and use the back stairs to get close enough to hear. Technically I am Underboss and engaged to the Don's daughter so I have no reason to hide. Well, no reason other than I don't want to be dragged into the drama.

I have enough of it going on with Elena and I's blossoming relationship, as well as the plans for the Cartel and last remaining rats in our ranks.

Ravinia is ripping into Bosco. He is trying to calm her down and tell her he found his first wife. That she wasn't dead. Which makes his marriage to herself illegitimate.

Shit. Their screaming is getting louder. Thank god the mansion walls are thick and nestled on fifty acres. Otherwise I don't doubt the neighbors would have heard and called the cops.

While Ravinia continues to scream, I watch as Elena comes up the stairs to see what the commotion is about. She's still in a pair of my clothes and damn do I love seeing her that way. So does my dick. Not now buddy. I had a closet full of clothes delivered a few days ago and put in our room. She's worn the jeans and sweatshirts. It seems at night she prefers to smell of me. I'd prefer her naked, but we'll get there.

Unlike me, Elena isn't hiding. The moment Ravinia sees her, she rushes over to her. "You. Who the hell are you?"

"I'm Elena. You must be Ravinia." She says it like she isn't positive. I stifle a laugh at the irony of her words. Elena knows exactly who she is. Hell she probably knows what Ravinia had for breakfast and when her last shit was. It's scary how much she has been able to learn about us, and all without us having the slightest clue.

Bosco moves to Elena's side. Guess I should probably make my appearance now too. I step out of the shadows and take position at Elena's other side.

"What is going on? Bosco who is this bitch?" Shrieks Ravinia.

Elena tenses. I'm sure she is biting her tongue so hard it's bleeding. I grab her hand. Lending her my strength. Or letting her take out her aggression.

Damn! She has my hand in a death grip. It's so tight her nails are digging into my skin. Thank god she doesn't have sharp, acrylic nails like Milan.

"Elena is my daughter." Bosco says proudly.

"What?!" Ravinia's jaw is dropped open.

"And my fiancé." I add.

"No!" She screams.

"Mom, what's going on?" Milan asks as she climbs down the stairs. It's two am and she has a tight dress and sky high heels on already. At least her makeup isn't as extravagant as it usually is. I'm guessing she rushed to throw an outfit on that was worthy of pleasing her mother before racing downstairs when she heard yelling. God forbid she was seen looking anything less than a plastic doll.

Milan takes notice of my hand in Elena's. "Luca? Who is this?"

I see Elena give me glance sideways before releasing my hand with a small nod. As though telling me to go to Milan and let her down easy. "Milan, why don't we talk in the library?" She smiles brightly and gives a glare to Elena. Her attitude change has me internally cringing. She thinks I am abandoning Elena in favor of her.

As we walk in silence, I mull over how to tell Milan that our arranged marriage is off. She has been looking forward to it for years. She has told all her friends. It's is going to crush her. I may not have wanted to marry her, but I never wanted to hurt her.

We settle onto one of the sofas. I try to keep a few feet between us. She quickly scoots closer. Her thigh pressed tightly against mine. Her hands grasping my forearm. I want to pull myself free. The unfamiliar feeling of betraying Elena crawls along my skin. I try to shake the thought. Elena has a heart. She will know that Milan needs this. Needs me. Her world is about to be turned upside down. I'm not usually one to show emotion or comfort another. Elena is the first to have seen it. The first to experience it. For her it comes naturally to me.

Damn. What is happening to me?

I need to grow my balls back after this. I'm going to be Don. We are at war with the Cartel. This sappy crap needs to be kept under wraps. Except for my Elena. I will soak her in affection as I ravage her body in our bed. She will be what I fight to come home to each night. Not that she will be waiting for me. I'm sure my little hellcat will be stepping into the house with me. She isn't one to sit back and let others take charge. She will want to be in on the action and I will be powerless to stop her. Not that I will want to. Elena has already proven herself capable of holding her own in a fight. Besides, with her by my side I can keep an eye on her better than trusting her to stay at home.

I'm going to have my hands full keeping her in line. Teaching her to work with others. Work with me. Beside me.

I look forward to the challenge.

I have to be cautious not to let the smile I feel tingle my cheeks show. This conversation with Milan is serious. Smiling as I destroy all that she has believed to be true is a dick move even for me.

Turning to her. I separate our legs and take her hands into my own. I need her focus on the words coming out of my mouth. Not on her hands creeping up my bicep.

"Milan." I take a deep breath. Making sure I have her attention. "Things around here are going to be changing. A lot of things actually."

A smile crosses her face. She leans in closer with her chest. "You mean me and you? I'm ready Luca. I've been ready. I know you wanted to wait until I turn eighteen. You don't have to." I see the hope and desire in her eyes and realize I've already screwed this conversation up. "I mean legally I need to be sixteen to marry and my mom and dad will need to sign off…"

I shake my head. "Milan, that's not what I'm talking about."

"You're not?" The disappointment flashes across her face before she is able to hide it. She plasters on the smile Ravinia taught her.

"This is difficult for me to tell you. I want you to know though, this changes nothing with Bosco. You understand?"

"Luca. Whatever it is I can handle it. I am the daughter of the Don." If she only knew. Well, soon she will.

"Before your father married your mom, he had another wife." Her eyes widen. "When he was eighteen they married. A few weeks later she disappeared. He was told she died."

Her hand covers her mouth. Gone is the mask her mom has ingrained in her to wear. "Oh my god. That's horrible."

"It was. Until a few days ago." Her hand slowly lowers

107

back to her lap. "Her name is Violet. And she's alive."

"That's wonderful!" There is genuine excitement in her voice.

"And she has a daughter." I wait to see if Milan understands. She doesn't. "Bosco's daughter. She was pregnant when she was forced to flee the city."

Her eyes stray away from me. The brightness in them not yet diminished like I feared. "I have a sister?"

I smile at her. Trying my best to reassure her before her world truly collapses. "Her name is Elena. She's here."

"She is! Can I meet her? I always wanted a sister. Do you think she will like me?" Milan jumps up from the couch. Her hands smoothing down her dress and fluffing up her hair. All the things I've noticed over the years that she does before entering a room.

"Of course. She's excited to meet you too." Her nervous primping calms. I stand and grab her hands again. "That's not all though. Let's sit."

Following my lead, we fall back to the couch. She is more distant with her body than before. She must see the hesitation in my eyes. "Is it bad? You've got that look. The same one dad has when he doesn't want to tell me something." I would laugh if this wasn't so serious. In recent years I have noticed myself becoming more and more like Bosco. It's not a bad thing. He's a great boss. All the soldiers respect him. He is fair even in his punishments.

"Not bad. Or it doesn't have to be. Nothing needs to change."

"Luca. I don't understand. Why would me having a sister potential make things bad?"

Stealing another breath. "Violet and Bosco are still legally married. It means the marriage to your mother isn't." Her face doesn't change. I don't think she understands. Fuck.

Bosco should be the one telling her this shit.

Ravinia is still screaming. Her voice is echoing down the hall and into the room even with the door shut. Yeah. Maybe it's better I am in here with Milan than dealing with that witch. I would be struggling not to tie her up and gag her. It's sad how much of a scene she is making. She is supposed to be the Queen of the Mafia.

Internally I smile again. Elena would never make a scene like that. In private I have no doubt she wouldn't unleash on me. I'm looking forward to it. I'll take her anger as long as I get her pleasure afterwards.

From the little I have learned about Violet, she would be like Elena. Quiet. Calculating. And handling shit with a scary calmness.

I need to finish this conversation. It won't make things easier by dragging it on. "Bosco has already contacted the Council. They are moving forward with recognizing Elena as his firstborn."

"Okay." Her brow furrows. She knows this is an important detail. She just hasn't figured out why yet.

"That means our marriage contract is void. I am to marry Elena."

Milan jumps up. She backs across the room. "No." Her head is shaking back and forth. I can tell she doesn't want to believe what I've said. "No. No. They can't do that. You're mine. They already agreed." I take a step forward. I want to comfort her. She's still just a kid. There's no way she understands what marriage would be like. Much less a loveless marriage to me.

Even if she was old enough, I wouldn't love her. It would have been a sad truth she would have tried to deny. Much like Ravinia denies it with Bosco. He cares for her health and safety, but there is no love there. His heart has always belonged to Violet. Even when he thought her dead.

Violet's only been in his life again for a few days and already he has changed. I recognize those changes in myself. The moment I met Elena I felt the ice around my heart thaw. Years ago I had thought I'd marry for love, then I signed the marriage contract to Milan and my heart froze. I built a barrier around my emotions so no woman would get close. It would have been cruel for me to fall in love when I would not be able to give them a marriage and babies. A short lived fling would have been all I would have been capable of.

Elena changed that. She is unlike any woman I have ever met. The fact that she is Bosco's heir allows my heart to beat again. I'm not at risk of hurting her by leaving her. I'm not allowed to.

There will be no running by either of us. The foundation of lust is already there. The walls of respect and admiration are building. Soon she will love me. I won't accept anything less. For years I had been resigned to never knowing love between husband and wife. Never looking forward to waking up to the same woman day after day. Seeing her belly grow with my child knowing it was a product of love and not duty.

Before I can pull Milan into my arms the door opens. I hadn't notice Ravinia's screaming stop. Bosco enters first. Followed by Massimo, Val, my father and Elena trailing behind.

"You!" Milan shouts and tries to rush at Elena. I move quickly and wrap an arm around Milan's waist. I pull her back to my chest. She fights to free herself from my hold. "You ruined everything! Luca was supposed to be mine!"

Elena doesn't say anything. To her credit she doesn't cower or run from the room either. The desire is there in her eyes, so is sadness. Elena had said she had once been excited to have a sister. Any hope of them having a relationship is quickly crumbling.

"Milan. Stop." Orders Bosco. He crosses the room in four steps. He cups Milan's face in his hands. Instantly she calms enough for me to let her go. She sags against her father.

"It's not fair." She sobs into his chest.

I move closer to Elena. Tears are pooling in her eyes. At first I wonder if they are from Milan's words.

No. The tears are for the bond Milan and Bosco share. The bond of a father and daughter that have grown together. The bond Elena doesn't have. She could. It will never be the same as Milan's. Though that doesn't mean it can't be just as strong. Bosco loves Elena. He didn't have to change her diaper or teach her to ride a bike to love her. Protecting her mother, breaking into the compound, shooting Santo and tracking down their enemies, those are the moments he has seen and admires. More moments will come later. Hopefully Elena will be willing to open her heart to Bosco and let him share them.

In silent support I wrap my arm around her shoulders and pull her close. She doesn't lean into me. I wasn't expecting her to. She is working double time to rebuild her walls.

Not going to happen baby girl.

"I'm sorry pumpkin." Elena tenses further at his term of endearment for Milan. "In order for Luca to be Don, he must marry my heir. Elena is four years older than you. That right is hers." Milan sobs harder. Her head still shaking back and forth in disagreement.

CHAPTER FIFTEEN

Elena

Pumpkin.

He calls her pumpkin.

If Santo hadn't of threatened mom, would I have been his pumpkin?

I'm already fighting back tears. The feel of Luca's arm wrapping around me isn't helping. He wants me to know I can crumble. I can break and he will hold me together. The deepest parts of me wants to. I want to so badly I am nearly trembling at the thought.

I have been the only one to hold myself together for so long. What would it be like to allow someone else in? To let them carry some of the burden.

I want that.

I can't.

My mom trusted the family once. She trusted Bosco and look where it lead her. Twenty years on the run. No friends, no family. Sleeping in dingy apartments and flea invested motels. Living off of noodles and peanut butter and jelly sandwiches. Nearly dying because she couldn't see a doctor until it was nearly too late.

My tears dry quickly. I won't fall for their false promises. Look what it's doing to Milan. For years she has believed she would marry Luca. She had her heart set on it. Now she is crushed and that burden falls to me.

I sneak a peek at Luca. He has dark circles starting under his eyes. The hard plains of his chest are felt against my arm and back from where he is pressing against me. Marrying him isn't a burden in theory. He is gorgeous. He makes me laugh. Makes me want to trust.

He's dangerous. Not just because of his role in the mafia. No. The threat is to my heart. If I let my walls down I would fall head over heels for him. Worse than Milan because I know he feels for me too. Our sexual chemistry is off the charts. Just standing near him has me wanting to rub my thighs together.

I can't allow him to burrow himself any deeper and stir up more feelings. I need a plan.

He says if I run he will hunt me down. I have no doubt that he would. Luca is anything if not determined. Relentless. I've seen it with his mission against the Cartel. If his body and mind didn't cease to be useful after days without sleep I'm sure he'd never rest.

Would Ronan be able to help me? Could he help me get away? I'd only need a little head start. Running for so long gives you a bag full of tricks.

I could fake my death again. Would Luca believe it? He would want a body. Undeniable proof.

Crap.

My mind whirls as I tune one ear back to Bosco and Milan. He's stroking her hair and murmuring into her ear. I feel like a fraud. We're intruding on their moment.

"Yes papa." She says to him as she raises her eyes to him and wipes the tears away. His face looks heartbroken. Would he look the same when I leave? Would he care because he cares for me, or would he be upset that I left him with no heir? It would start a war.

Shit. Can I leave knowing I'd send the family into civil war? There would be casualties. Would Bosco or Luca be one of them?

What about my mom? She's happy here. I can't ask her to leave again.

"I love you Milan. I will always love you and be here for you. This changes nothing. You are my daughter. I don't care what the tests say."

He told her. He told her about her true parentage. How did I miss that? How long have I been lost in my own head?

She looks heartbroken. I knew it would crush her. I didn't want it to. During the time I spent observing everyone I grew to like Milan. Not the version her mom designed. No, the one she hides in her bedroom. The one who spends her days reading physics books and taking on-line advanced literature classes. The dumb blond that she portrays in public is anything but the truth. She is brilliant.

I have long admired her strength and her commitment to her mother. Just like my love for my mother, Milan would do anything to make her mother happy and proud of her.

A small part of me had hoped we could be friends, one day even sisters. It was silly to hope. A sad dream I allowed myself to have knowing I can't let anyone close.

"Do you know who my father is?" Milan asks. Her voice is soft. Different than usual. The mask Ravinia trained her to wear is gone. The true Milan is out and I doubt the mask will ever reappear. Today is the start of a new life for Milan. From the shadows I will make sure she is happy. Bosco will make sure she is protected from the visible threats. Me, I will hunt the ghosts. I can't let her close to me, but I can do this for her. Like I've been doing for the family since I first learned of my father's identity years ago.

"I do." Bosco continues to stroke her hair. "He's here. He's always been here. He didn't know until today either. Would you like to see him?" Bosco must see the struggle in her eyes. "You don't have to. He knows you may not be ready."

"Will he like me?"

Ricco steps forward. "He does. He's proud of the woman you are. He didn't know you were his, but he's always been close."

"He has?" Milan's face lights up with interest.

Bosco nods to Massimo who slides out the door. No doubt going to get Mario. "I won't leave your side. Like I said. This changes nothing between us. I'm still you dad."

"What if he wants a relationship with me too?"

"Then you have it. I won't stop you. He and I have already spoken. We understand this is big news to you. To all of us. We both want what is best for you. If you want us both in your life, both as your dads, then we are. If you want me to back off so you can get to know him…" He doesn't get to finish. Milan relaunches into his arms.

Massimo returns with Mario.

"Never. I don't want you to go anywhere."

Bosco places a kiss to her forehead. "Then I won't." He pulls her back a little so he can wipe her tears. "Ready?" She hasn't seen Mario yet.

He hadn't known the truth about her until earlier today. We're not sure if Ravinia even knew.

Mario had admitted to being seduced by Ravinia one night when he was on guard at the penthouse. Mario had been so guilty that he betrayed the boss that he considered turning himself in for punishment for months. It wasn't until Ravinia had learned she was pregnant that he knew he could never come clean. And he never allowed Ravinia to get her claws in him or any other guard again. Mario had said that Bosco was happy to be expecting a child that he couldn't spoil the news with the knowledge of Ravinia's adultery.

Bosco forgave him quickly. He knew what Ravinia was like. How she was when she got an idea in her head. If Bosco didn't care for Milan the way he did, I have no doubt that his attitude towards Mario would be different. Bosco hid it well but the betrayal cut him deep. A mafia man would want retribution. For Milan he was letting it go. She deserved to get to know her biological father.

It's strange. Mario had been Milan's guard since she was an infant. He had held her the day she was born and never knew it was his child he held.

Fuck.

I feel the tears build in my eyes again. She had two fathers all along. Milan and Mario hadn't known the truth but Mario had always been by her side. I had seen it before even I knew the truth. He was more than a guard to her. He was more like an uncle.

Milan peaks around Bosco's broad shoulders. Her gaze travels the room. The land for a few seconds on me before they move on. "Mario?"

"Hi Milan." Mario stands stiffly by the door. It's easy to tell how nervous he is. She could reject him.

She doesn't.

She runs to him. "I'm glad it's you."

Mario visibly relaxes. His arms cradle Milan to his chest. "Me too. I would hate to have to share you with anyone else cupcake."

Bosco smiles contentedly at them. They were going to be just fine. All three of them.

CHAPTER SIXTEEN

Elena

While everyone was watching the new dynamic unfold between Bosco, Milan, and Mario I slipped out of Luca's hold and made my way back to the basement. I couldn't watch anymore. It hurt too much. Milan had a relationship with two dads while I had none. Even if I let Bosco in now, it would be too late. He didn't help raise me. He didn't get to pick me up when I fell down. I didn't have dance recitals he could attend, or monsters under the bed he could slay.

I had bigger monsters. Ones that I had to fight myself long before any kid should have had to. I know it's not his fault. He didn't know I existed.

Still. It hurts.

As I round the corner to where Mom's make-shift hospital room is, I am hit again with the reality of my upbringing.

I don't have a family. Not truly. Even on the run for twenty years mom hasn't been forgotten from hers. I watch on as she laughs with her parents. The grandparents I never knew, who still have made no real effort to get to know me. Not that I blame them. I've been busy. Plus, I don't know what to say.

We have nothing in common. My grandmother likes to garden. We never stayed anywhere long enough for me to see a plant grow. Grandpa likes the Chicago Bears. I've never watched a football game.

For protection, my mother's extended family is here too. There are a dozen of them. Aunt, Uncles, and Cousins all catching mom up on what she missed the last two decades. I feel like a stranger watching them. I have no connection to them. Not really. The Violet they remember is not the Violet I was raised by. She had to change and adapt to protect me. Being with them again, I can see her changing, becoming the woman she was before we had to run. Her walls are dropping fast. The fear to hold people at arm's length is gone for her.

Pain radiates from my chest. She won't run again with me. This is the life she should have always had. She will be safe here. I'll make sure she is.

The Caruso family Doctor is going to do the Kidney transplant tomorrow morning and oversee her and my Aunt's recover. Mom had two matches in the family. They both agreed to donate. After a brief playful fight Aunt Jenna won.

I need to make sure it is safe for her. I need to finish the job I started. There are still a few names on my list. I need to take care of them. The Cartel needs to be stopped.

I stay in the shadows of the room observing. No one notices me. I like it that way. My mind is free to plan.

Hours later, the room clears. It's early morning. The people in the house should be waking up, instead everyone is going to bed. The events of the last few days has disrupted everyone's schedules. Soon it will go back to normal. It has to. I won't accept anything less. My mom deserves normal again.

My grandfather pats my shoulder as he walks by and up the stairs. I'm glad he didn't talk. I wouldn't have known what to say. My mind is a mess. Only vengeance is clear.

Mom is sitting up in her bed. She looks tired. I want to curl into her arms like I did as a child. I want her to wrap me in her warmth and believe her when she says we are safe for the night. It was always just for the night. She couldn't guarantee beyond it.

I'll make sure she doesn't have to worry beyond the night.

I try to settle into the seat closest to her. The mask I wear is firmly in place. I can't let her know my plan. Can't let her panic about what I am about to do. She needs to be calm and relaxed before her surgery. I don't want her worrying.

"I can hear those wheels in your head grinding sweetie." The corner of my mouth twitches. "What are you thinking so hard about?"

I won't lie to her. I won't tell the truth either. "Just hoping your surgery goes well tomorrow."

"It will." There is no doubt in her voice. Good. "And soon I will be feeling back to my old self." I nod. She won't be her old self. At least not the one I knew. That Violet is gone. "That's not it is it?"

Shit. I had hoped she would leave it at that. Still I have more I can say that still will prevent me from lying directly. "Bosco wants me to marry Luca."

"What?" I wondered if Bosco had said anything. Guess not.

I relax back into the chair. My eyes still flitting to the stairs. I'm not a fan of the basement. There is only one entrance and exit. Not helpful when you need a fast escape. "Says he needs a male heir to take over. Since he doesn't have a blood male then his female blood heir needs to marry the would be Don." Mom's gaze sits heavily on me. "Dad already chose Luca. Actually he had chose him to marry Milan, but since I'm here…" I can't help the huff of frustration that escapes my lips.

"You don't want to marry Luca?" Her surprise throws me. Does she want me to marry Luca?

"I don't want to marry anyone." At least I didn't. Luca would make a good husband. Or so I imagine. Definitely a great lover. I just can't allow myself to want it.

"You can't keep running." She says.

I know. Doesn't mean I won't try. "Why not? It served us well so far."

Mom scoots up further in the bed. Her body angling towards me. Her eyes are stern. "Yes, out of necessity. It's no way to live life." She believes it. She always has.

The difference between me and her is that she knows the difference. I don't. "It's the only life I know."

"Yes." There is a crack in her voice. Tears roll down her cheeks. Shit. I didn't want to upset her. "And that is my fault."

"No." I say as powerfully as I can without raising my voice. I need her to understand me. To believe me when I say, "don't you dare blame yourself. It was Santo. Santo threatened you."

"And that threat is over." She is trying to reassure me that I can stop running.

"Hardly." I grab her hand and stroke my thumb over the back of her hand. The same way she did to me each night as a child. "There is a crazed hit-man out to get us as well as a pissed off Cartel. The hospital was just the first step."

"Your father will handle it." Her naivety to see the truth pisses me off.

"Like he did when you went missing?" It's a low blow. It's also the truth.

"That's not fair."

I drop her hand and raise from the chair. I need to move. My blood is pumping too fast to sit. "Isn't it? He was told you left. Gave his ring back and ran away and got run off the road?" I hear my voice rising. I can't stop it. "A man in love would have gone after you. A husband wouldn't have let you go easy and a man with an entire army of men at his back should have used every resources and dollar available to find you or at the least avenged you. There should have been a trail or carnage in his wake. Instead what did he do?" I pause my pacing to look at her so I can use finger quotes. "He 'mourned' you with a picture in his desk drawer then waited a few years before remarrying. It's pathetic. He's pathetic."

"Elena!"

"No mom." Shit. I need to get out of here. I've already said more than I wanted to say. While everything I said is the truth, she didn't need to hear it. After the life we have had she deserved to live in her bubble of happiness longer. "He may have donated his sperm to create me, but I owe him nothing. In fact I want to burn his kingdom to the ground. He doesn't deserve to be Don!" All the pain and anger I felt the last few days is reaching a tipping point. I didn't deserve to have all this shit rubbed in my face. Milan's two dads, Luca's lust, Bosco and my mom's love, or her family's reunited happiness.

I've never gotten to be happy. I've never gotten a day's rest.

"Elena!" She yells louder. I stop my pacing. My hands grip my hair as I try to hold onto my sanity. "Look. I get it, you're mad. I am too. Don't you think I wanted my husband all these years? Don't you think I wanted him there for every birthday and holiday? I may not be the most domesticated woman but even I longed to greet him at the door with his slippers and glass of whiskey. I wanted someone I could shoulder the responsibilities with. I wanted someone to hold me when life got hard, and I wanted to be the shoulder he leaned on all these years." She pauses to take a breath. If she's trying to calm me down she is doing a shit job. She's just reiterating all the shit that could have been but never was. "I can't go back in time. If I could have, I would have done it. I don't know why he didn't come after me. I don't know why he didn't search harder or longer. Whatever the reason, I love him.

"I always have. He may only be my husband on paper now and maybe we'll leave when this is over, but I will never not love him. That love is the only thing that kept me going all these years."

The air shifts in the room. Someone else is here. I hadn't realized I let my back face the entrance. I know better. It's dangerous to be off guard.

It's Bosco. "I still love you too. Always have."

I want to call bullshit. I want to so bad. He didn't come for us.

Then it hits me. The words she said. "He's the only reason you kept going?" I didn't mean for the words to slip out of my mouth. Pain clutches my chest. My palm rubs a circle over it. As if I could soothe it. There is no soothing it.

Mom suddenly looks horrified. "That's not what I meant Elena." She reaches for me but I back away.

"No I think it is." All this time I was fighting for her. Thinking we were a team. Twenty years after he failed her and he still comes first. Did she only love me because I was a piece of him, the reminder she got to carry with her?

"Elena." Bosco moves to come towards me. I can't be touched. I don't want comfort or apologies. The betrayal my heart feels is nearly sending me to my knees. I never had friends. I only ever had my mom. Guess I was wrong. She was only ever Bosco's. Stupid.

"I need to go." Circling in a wide arch around Bosco so he can't grab me. I give her a kiss on the cheek. Her truth hurts. I'll get over it. I've gotten good at hiding my feelings and building walls. Never thought I needed to build them from her.

"No. We need to talk about this. I didn't mean it."

"It's okay mom. I still love you." Mom relaxes into the bed. She must think I forgive her. That I've already forgotten the hurt. I move to the stairs. I have a clear exit to the door. I put one foot on the steps and turn to Bosco. "Take care of her." Then I'm gone. Running up the stairs.

The house is quiet except for their yelling. I slam the door shut and lock it. It won't stop them for long.

Mom is yelling for Bosco to stop me. I take a step back from the door. He slams against it. It rattles but doesn't budge. It's too secure to move.

"Elena." He shouts. "Elena, open this door." I don't. I move farther away. "Elena, don't you dare leave. Your mother needs you!"

He keeps screaming. It disappears behind me as I race out the back door and down the lawn.

CHAPTER SEVENTEEN

Luca

Bosco paces in his office. Elena has been missing for two days and there are three Cartel bodies that have been found across the city. She's going to get herself killed. "What the hell is she thinking?" I am fuming. She left me. The hell-cat ran and I haven't been able to find her. Not that I haven't tried. I have all my men out searching and I have spent the last sixteen hours in a car driving around town aimlessly looking for any sign of her.

I have to hand it to her. She is good at disappearing when she wants to. It won't stop me. I will find her and bring her to heel and accept my help. She has to know she isn't alone anymore.

"She's thinking that her mother wants me more than her." Says Bosco glumly.

"That's ridiculous." I scoff.

"I know that. Violet said some stuff in the heat of the moment that isn't true. Elena didn't take it well. She saw it as a betrayal. Now she's hell-bent on finishing her revenge."

Bosco falls to his chair. His hands ringing his hair like he can pull the stress from its tips. "She's convinced I don't want her. That I already have a daughter and now that I have her mother back, that that's it." He leans back and lets his hands fall from his hair. I've never seen the boss look so defeated. "She thinks she lost her mother to me, and we don't have love for her too."

"Why would she think that I thought she was close to her mom? What did her mom say that had her second guessing her?" Pipes in Massimo. He's been by my side every minute since Elena ran out the back door. He hasn't slept. He's worried about her. He knows how much I have come to care about her. The bastard has hounded me about how I'm acting like a love sick puppy. He wouldn't know how I feel. He wasn't raised in a loving home like me. His heart isn't frozen. It is missing. Gone. A black hole. I'd feel sorry for him, if it didn't make him such an effective enforcer.

It's funny how a girl who thinks she has no one and runs because of it, actually has an entire family behind her. The soldiers that have crossed paths with her admire and respect her. She leaves an impression on people. Me more than anyone. I love her strength and fire. I just want it beside me, not running from me. I swear the girl is giving me gray hair and we haven't even married yet.

"Violet says they are, or were close." Bosco looks lost as he tries to explain. "She didn't mean it. Violet said I was the only reason she fought and ran all these years. Elena took it as her mom not doing it for her. I saw it in her eyes. The moment the words were out Elena broke. She thinks her mother doesn't care for her." Tears well in his eyes. The hardened Mafia Boss is crying. Fuck. I don't blame him. This situation is fucked. What Violet said is fucked. "Elena doesn't trust easy. We've all seen it firsthand. The only one she trusted was her mom. A split second was all it took to break it. My daughter didn't deserve this shit life. Now she's gone and I don't know where she is or how to show her she can trust us."

Massimo, who has remained mostly quiet the last few days, chimes in. "Even if we find her. How can we get her to stay? She is our heir. Her place is here. She doesn't see it. How can she not see that we want her here?"

To my surprise it is Val that responds. "I think she does see it. I think it scared her."

"Explain." I ask.

He nods before continuing. "She told us she has been on the run since the day she was born. I imagine that doesn't allow you to bond with anyone. Does she have any friends? I haven't heard her talk about anyone. The only one I know of that she has talked to is that Luna person. And even she hasn't spoken to her since the hospital incident."

"I haven't heard her talk to anyone outside this house since we got here." I say recalling my observations with her.

"She's been feeling trapped. Smothered. For nineteen years it has been just her and Violet. Now she has all of us. Even on our best days we are a lot to handle." We all laugh at Val's admission. He isn't wrong. We are a rowdy aggressive bunch.

"When we find her, we need to show her we are on her side. We can't crowd her though. And Luca…" Massimo singles me out. "She needs to finish her list. We know it's what she's doing. She's getting revenge on all those that threatened her mom all these years. When you see her you can't go all alpha caveman on her and force her to heel."

"I wasn't planning on it." I admit only to myself that the thought had crossed my mind. "I don't want to cage her. I want to protect her. She may be your daughter Bosco and technically our marriage has been arranged by you and the council, but I love her." Shit. I love her? What the hell? I barely know her.

No. I do know her. I don't know the finer details like what her favorite color or what movies she likes. What I know is her passion, her ambition, her strength and her fight. That's what I love. I don't want to smother her. I want to help her blossom into the Mafia Queen she was born to be.

Bosco perks up at my declaration. "You love my daughter?"

"I do. I know she's hurt and fragile right now. I'm not going to break her further. I am going to win her trust. By the time I'm done she will come home willingly."

Massimo snorts. "You realize you are going to have one hell of a fight before that right? And I don't just mean verbally. I heard about the ass kicking she already gave you. She is trained in some kind of defensive martial arts. Not to mention she's good with a gun and not afraid to shoot too."

"Yeah she is." My smile reaches my eyes thinking about her skills. When was the last time I smiled like this?

"You sick fuck. You are getting hard thinking about fighting your wife?"

Bosco clutches his hands to his ears. "Ugh. No. Stop. That's my daughter. She and I aren't close but there is no way in hell I want to hear anything to deal with your cock or intimacy with my daughter. Just no!" Massimo the bastard laughs at Bosco's discomfort.

"So what can we do? How do we stop or find her?" Asks Ricco.

"Her mother gave me a contact before she went into surgery. He is coming here. Apparently he met them both years ago. Ex-military. Likes to live off the grid. And the fucker taught her everything she knows."

"Is he a hacker?" Asks Val from the corner. His nose back down where it has been in his laptop since the alarm sounded when Elena left. He is hacking traffic and ATM cameras looking for her. Anything he can get into with a camera or microphone he is checking. We thought we had a lead six hours ago. The body we found was cold when we got there. I know it was Elena. She is falling down the rabbit hole and if we don't find her soon, I don't know if we will be able to pull her out. Taking a life whether warranted or not hurts the soul. We need to find her. I won't stop her. I know she needs this to feel safe. The Caruso family needs to be safe.

Santo screwed us big time. Elena may become our savior and I hate it. The burden is too much for one person. It's why our organization has levels. Counterparts that help shoulder the responsibilities. As Don and Underboss the burden should fall to Bosco and I. Elena has taken it out of our hands and she is trying to carry it alone. I don't want her to stumble. I can't risk her tripping up. She is in the lion's den. One wrong move and the Cartel will capture and torture her. They don't follow the same laws that we do. They aren't above hurting women.

"No. Apparently she's mainly self-taught in that department." Replies Bosco.

"She has to have someone that's helping her with it. There's no way she hacked those cars and lights while we were chased. She's good but she can't be that good." Val's fingers stop typing. I'm not sure they've stopped all day. The frustration Val feels at his inability to track her digitally can be read all over his face. It's how we all feel. Defeated. Still, none of us plan on giving up. I told her if she ran I would chase and I would burn the world down if I need to.

Maybe that's the answer. Instead of trying to track Elena, we need to track the Cartel. She's after them anyway. At some point we will either cross her path or the Cartel will run out of men and maybe then she will come home.

"I agree but her mom doesn't know who that would be." I try to tune back into their conversation even though my mind has moved onto her next possible target. "Is there any way you can find out? If they are her friend maybe they know where she is or can help us track her."

Val gives a nod of his head and turns back to his computer. He doesn't get two buttons pushed before the bottom of it is smoking. "What the hell!" He flips it on its side and goes to remove the battery.

His screen goes red. A message appears. *You won't find me or Elena if she doesn't want to be found.*

Holy shit! Someone was listening to us. Was this her friend? Is Elena with her?

"Elena? Elena where are you?" I'm shouting at the cameras on the ceiling. "We want to help!"

The red screen flashes again. The smoke has stopped. *She doesn't want help.*

"Who are you? Are you a friend?" Damn I feel stupid having a conversation between the ceiling and a computer screen.

I'm Luna. Before I can ask another question, I have a hundred for this Luna person, the screen flashes another message before there is a pop and the screen goes black. *Elena needs to do this her way.*

Fuck. She can do it her way. I just want to be there so I can protect her. If she would rather personally burn the world down than me, I'll give her the damn match and toss the gasoline.

It is quiet in the room. None of us speak. Val looks like he wants to cry. He doesn't. I would understand if he did. He isn't built like the rest of the men in the family. Val is emotional. It serves him well in his role. No one would dare pick on him for it. He isn't built to be an enforcer. He needs to read people. Know their secrets and use it to blackmail them. Elena has been a puzzle he can't figure out and now this Luna has taken out the tool he needed most to find her.

Sure he has other computers. In fact he already has a new one fired up and running. Who knows though if Luna will trash this one too?

I hate threats I can't see. That I don't know. What the hell happened to old fashion fist fights?

There is a knock at the door. Bosco calls them in. I don't recognize the man. He is about six foot five with long hair pulled back in loose bun. He looks ready for battle with his combat boots, cargo pants, and guns on his hips. The all black outfit would look menacing to the average person. Not us. All eyes are on him as he crosses the room to stand before Bosco.

"Mr. Caruso, so kind of you to invite me to your home? To what do I owe the pleasure?" His voice is calm. His posture is not. He is on edge. He has good reason to be. There are five of us in the room all armed to the teeth.

"Ronan, welcome. It's about Elena."

The man's face instantly changes. "What's wrong? What happened to her?" The sincerity in his voice is evident.

"Nothing. At least nothing that we know of."

"What is that supposed to mean? You're her father? Shouldn't you know?"

"She told you?" I can't disguise my surprise.

"Violet told me. It's why I agreed to help her all those years ago. Her car had died on the side of the road. She had been trying to make it to the hospital. One of your men had attacked her in her home and she had run as quick as she could. The stress caused her to go into labor." He pauses and moves to the window. "Pregnant and alone on the side of the road." His eyes go blank as though he can see the memory before him.

"You were there?" I already know the answer. The question slips out anyway.

"I helped her deliver Elena and wrapped her in my jacket." Multiple emotions shimmer in his eyes. He cares for them. Both of them.

"What is your relationship with Violet?" Bosco looks tense again as he speaks. Actually he looks ready to throw a fist at Ronan.

"Relax Don." He says taking a step back. "Violet is a friend. I love her but not in that way. Elena on the other hand, she is the closest thing I will ever have to a daughter." His face turns down. "Not that she willingly lets me. She holds everyone at a distance. Even me."

Fuck. If she holds him at a distance how helpful is he going to be?

"Yes, we've seen how un-trusting she can be."

"Wouldn't you be?" It's clear Ronan holds a grudge against Bosco. He doesn't know him personally. His opinion is derived from the words and feelings of Violet and Elena. "Her mother and her have been running for their lives for two decades. Elena has never known stability. Her mother did her best but…" Ronan pauses. His eyes turn to me. Does he know of my relationship with Elena? That I am contracted to marry her. His eyes don't give away the answer. "Elena has scars. Physically, mentally, and emotionally. She may never trust you." He breaks eyes contact with me. "Any of you."

The fire in me that died from my lack of sleep is building again. "I can't just leave her out on the streets. She's pissed off the Cartel and if she keeps up this vigilante shit then I fear she might piss of the Russians or Irish as well."

Ronan laughs. He fucking laughs. "You underestimate Elena."

"I don't know her well enough yet not to."

"And you think I do?" The laughter is still in his eyes.

"I think you trained her. So you might be able to find her."

"Perhaps." He says with a shrug.

"What will it take?" Asks Bosco.

I'm not sure I like the smile that crosses his face.

CHAPTER EIGHTEEN

Elena

The hit-man, Edward "Sharp" Johnson, is three feet in front of me. He doesn't know I'm here. The knife in my hand is warm against my skin. Dried with the blood of six men, it hasn't left my hand all day. Three more are strapped to my thigh. I've got a gun in the back of my pants.

I won't use it. Not unless I have to. These men have fucked with my life for too long. I need to feel their blood on my hands. I need to feel the thrum of their pulse as their heart beats them dry.

This asshole is going down. He hadn't been able to be recalled before Santo died. He was a contract killer. Paid in advance to not stop until either the target was dead, or he was. Santo had been reckless and led me to him. Old bastard should have learned to wipe his hard-drive. Suppose I shouldn't be too mad. I now get to check this one off my list quicker than I thought.

Over the last two days I had been setting a trail of breadcrumbs for him to find me that led to my "Safe House".

It was an abandoned house on the outskirts of town. I didn't want any innocent people harmed. I also didn't want to be interrupted.

This man needed to be put down. First, I needed info. I needed to know that no one else was coming for us. Then I could move on. Only a handful of top brass of the Cartel remained in town and they were scared. Scared men made mistakes. Mistakes got you killed.

After that I could leave town. My mother had my dad and her family. She wouldn't be lonely anymore and she wouldn't need to run.

Yeah. That was best.

I could keep an eye on her from a distance. Maybe even come back to town every few months.

But I couldn't stay. I couldn't get sucked into the family business. The bloodshed and fighting wasn't a problem. It was having someone else dictate my life. Bosco telling me who to marry and not allowing me out of the house. Luca forcing me to talk and to feel. I couldn't do it. I couldn't pretend to fit into their world.

I couldn't be surrounded by so many people. I would always be paranoid. Growing up it had been a necessity. It wasn't something I could turn off. It was best to leave. Luca would go back to marrying Milan.

The idea instantly had my stomach twisting into knots. I didn't want to admit it but I didn't just have a crush on Luca. I was falling for him. Started long before I broke in to the mansion. He had intrigued me from the first day I started surveying the Caruso family. His darkness called to mine. I wasn't always dark, only when I needed to be. When I was threatened or hunted. Luca was darkest when he was on a job. When he was hanging out with Val or Massimo he dropped his guard. He would smile, laugh, and joke.

Watching the three of them was the longest I had ever observed how a friendship worked.

It made me jealous. Especially knowing that could have been my life. Should have been.

If Santo hadn't run my mom off, would Luca and I have dated like a normal couple? Would I have had late nights hanging with the boys shooting pool and sharing secrets only Mafia kids know?

Shit. I wanted Luca. I wanted him bad. I wanted to hear him laugh. I wanted him to teach me pool like he taught Val. I wanted to go on a date with him. I wanted the full package.

No. I tried to shake the thought away. He wasn't mine to have. He needed to be Milan's.

Bosco hadn't told the Council about her true parentage. No one would. It was a closely guarded secret. One I would take steps to ensure stayed that way. There is no reason to not believe she is his daughter. They will marry as originally planned. Then Luca can become Don. Everyone is happy. Everything is as it should be.

So why am I not happy?

Focus Elena! Kill this asshole, wrap up the Cartel, and I can go find my happiness.

Eddy takes another step forward. He's being cautious. I would admire him for it, if I didn't want to hurry this along. My trap was set in front of him. I give a hard shove at his back. He stumbles forward. Completely caught off guard. The rope snaps around his ankles and swings him into the air. He hangs upside down. The creaking of the old rafters tells me it won't hold him for long. No matter. My plans don't involve him being upside down for long.

I pull a syringe from my pocket and injected him in the neck. He should be asleep for an hour or so.

As I predicted, an hour later, he stirs. Within seconds he

is squirming against the straps I secured him with. The rope and zip types are biting into his skin. I can see small droplets of blood.

I'm sitting straddled in a backwards chair. I wait for him to speak first. Weak men always speak first.

"It seems you aren't as weak and vulnerable as your Uncle claimed you to be." Good boy for talking. Pathetic he didn't last longer.

"Santo is the weak one. Running off a pregnant teenager because he was threatened by her." I mock surprise. "She saw right through that asshole."

"And yet he was the right hand man of the Don for the last thirty years."

"They were blind. Too caught up in the notion of blood never turning on blood. It's all bullshit. Loyalty is so much more than blood."

"I agree."

"Why did you accept the hit?" The question had nagged me with each hit-man that came our way.

He gives a lick of his lips. He winces. I hit him a couple times while he was out. He just discovered his split lip. "Intrigue. Challenge I guess."

Interesting. "We were a challenge?" I ask.

"Would you disagree?"

"No. I just don't understand why you would admit it." I can see why intrigue would push him to take a hit on a woman and her kid. I'm equally intrigued by this man and what makes him tick. How he chooses his kills. If he is as good as Santo believed him to be, he would have his choice of any job.

"I may be a bad guy but I'm not a liar."

"Why do you do it?" Might as well ask my silly questions first while he's being open. I can torture him for the harder ones later.

"I just told you." He looks at me as though I am stupid.

Bad move buddy. I take a knife and jam it into his thigh. To his credit he doesn't utter a peep. "Not me specifically. Why do you kill in general?"

"Why do you?"

"Preservation and necessity."

"Necessity." He repeats it. He isn't asking a question though.

"Evil men deserve to be put down. The sacrifice of one is worth the safety of many."

"So you are judge and jury?"

The slight movement of his right hand catches my eye. He is trying to be discreet. My senses are on overload from all the adrenaline course through my veins. I notice every detail. He is trying to work the restraints loose while he plays into my questions.

I let him continue for another minute. Until he is making progress. I need to dampen his spirit a bit. Quicker than he can blink, I slam one of my knives through his right hand. The tip of my blade is firmly embedded in the wood of the chair arm. He won't be able to free it now without doing extensive damage to his hand.

He grunts but others wise doesn't make a sound.

"Don't fucking move again." I have questions and I intend to have answers to all of them.

Before I can ask another question, the door to the room slams open and clatters to the floor. Splinters scattering across the wood. I don't flinch. I knew Luca was getting close.

Fuckers just had to call in Ronan. The self-righteous asshole always hated my need for vengeance. He was always telling me that killing wasn't going to heal my soul. I was well aware. Nothing could heal it. I was too damaged. Be that as it may, it did sooth it temporarily.

Besides I wasn't going to kill forever. I had a list. One that was almost complete.

CHAPTER NINETEEN

Luca

Looking every bit the Mafia Queen she was, Elena stood over her tormentor. The man who had spent the last few years chasing her and her mother. The man who had personally marked her skin with a dozen scars.

She wasn't mine when it happened. The reminder doesn't calm my anger. I couldn't stop him from hurting her.

Elena has things under control. He can't hurt her anymore. She will end him. I won't interfere. It's not why I came. I came to watch her back. She's been doing it on her own for so long, it's time someone else stepped up to help.

I'll be damned if another man tries to do it. She is mine to protect. To marry. To fuck. Mine.

I scan over the man in the chair. My eyes need to confirm he is strapped down tight. Next I scan over Elena. She doesn't appear injured at all. She looks exhausted though. I wonder if she has gotten any sleep in the last few days.

Forgetting the man in the chair, I storm over to her and pull her into my arms. I need her close. I need my hands to feel she's real. She's here. My left arm brings her waist to mine. My right hand goes to her hair. I wrap it around my fingers and pull back. Using it to lead her head where I need it.

My lips descend on her. It isn't graceful. Fuck graceful. I wanted passionate. All consuming. I wanted to burn Elena with my desire.

After a few minutes I pull back. Together we pant and attempt to catch our breath.

"If you ever, ever, run from me like that again I will chain you to our bed for a month." I nip at her ear for effect.

"I am not your doll to do with as you please."

"Oh don't I know it." Keeping my tight grip on her, I walk her to the wall. With her sandwiched between the wall and myself, guards at the windows and doors, I feel the tension in my shoulders ease. Elena is safe. She's in my arms. Unhurt. "You are not a doll. You are a pain in the ass." Her jaw drops. It looks like she is getting ready to argue. I silence her with a kiss. "But you're my pain in the ass. You want vengeance you come to me."

"I don't need you to fight my battles."

"I never said that."

"Then what are you saying?"

"I'm saying that I will stand at your side. Hell I'll hand you the knife. I don't want to change you. I like how passionate you are. Maybe tone down the stubbornness a bit. Let down your walls so I can see into that gorgeous head of yours. But never, never do I want to hold you back. You going full vigilante and running from the house, that shit stops now. You aren't a lone wolf anymore. You have a family."

"They aren't...." She starts then quickly silences herself.

"They are. Me too." My eyes burrow their gaze into hers.

I need her to feel the sincerity in them.

"Not yet." She mumbles.

"Soon enough." I untangle my hands from her hair. I stroke her sharp jaw. "I protect my family. I protect what's mine, and you Elena, are mine!" I kiss her again. Less aggressive but no less full of passion.

The man in the chair is trying to get loose. My ears twitch against the near silent noise. I watch from my peripheral vision as he gets his legs free. I can feel Elena smile against my lips. My little psycho princess planned on him getting loose. She likes the fight.

I take her gun from her waistband and shoot the man in the knee. He screams. She pulls back from me. Looks at the man's wound, then me and back. I wonder what she is thinking. She didn't stop me. She doesn't look pissed.

"I wanted to shoot him first!" She says. I laugh. My Elena. Ever the Psycho Princess out for blood.

"How about you shoot him last?" Her eyes light up.

"You won't try to stop me?" She questions.

"Elena, when are you going to trust me? I told you. I'm not here to stop you. I want to stand beside you." I hand her back the gun. Together I turn us so we face the hit-man.

My hands are wrapped around her hips. My mouth kisses her shoulder as I pull her ass to settle against my hard cock. "When this one is dead, you and I need to discuss this list of yours."

"Not much of a list left." She says proudly.

Honestly. I'm proud of her too. "Regardless. You are too important to me to be running around the streets killing by yourself. And the paperwork and money exchanges that are required to keep it from getting out to the public is a nuisance. You are a Mafia Princess. Soon to be Queen. There are better ways to do this."

"I know." Not a hint of regret or desire to change in her voice. "They aren't as satisfying though." She lets out a huff. "Fine. He can be the last one."

"Good. I can't have you running around hunting bad guys while you're pregnant."

She gasps and puts a hand over her belly. "I'm not pregnant. We haven't even had sex yet." I scan her eyes. Looking for any sign that she is repulsed by the idea of kids with me. I don't see it. In fact she cradles her stomach as though she is already carrying our child.

"Not yet." I kiss her atop the nose.

"Who said I wanted kids?"

"You don't?"

"I do." She replies quickly.

"Then what's the problem?"

"What if I don't want them with you?" I growl at her playfulness. My hips thrusting into her so she can feel how hard I am for her.

"The only person you are having kids with is your husband, which in a few weeks will be me." I remind her.

"What if I don't want them now?"

"I'm not getting any younger babe, and the families need to know we'll have a blood heir for the next generation. They are grumbling enough about you coming out of nowhere and throwing them off their game." I'm lying. Sort of. We will need an heir. That part is truthful enough. Technically though, I can wait. I'm not yet thirty so I have time. I don't want to wait though. I want Elena bound to me in all ways.

"Ugh, fine. One kid." She waggles one finger in my face. I nip at it. She laughs.

"Four." I counter.

"Four?" She squeaks. "I'm not even sure I'm going to be a good mother to one."

"You will be. And I'll be by your side for it all. We don't need to be perfect. We just need to love them and keep them safe."

"That I can do."

"I know you can babe." I seal the deal with a kiss.

CHAPTER TWENTY

Elena

Luca refuses to let go of my hand. I think he thinks I am going to run off again. I won't. The hit-man is dead. The only one left that is a threat is the Cartel. Or more specifically, Ramirez.

He wants Chicago. He can't have it. They may not have been my target originally, but they certainly were once I found my dad and Luca. Whether I like it or not, I am the Princess of the Caruso Family. Or as Luca keeps reminding, the soon to be Queen. They threatened my family. They will pay.

I take slow steps into my mother's room. Luca told me the surgery was a success and that she was recovering. I'm not sure if I'm still mad at her. Her words hurt. I thought we were a team. I knew she had lingering feelings for Bosco. Not that I understood. I had never been in love. Not in that way.

Luca presses against my back. Silently encouraging me to get closer. My feet are planted firmly where they are. I don't want to talk to her yet. I just needed a peek at her. I needed to see with my own eyes that she was alive.

Bosco sits by her side. His Capos spread around the room. He's holding her hand. Looking at her the way I always imagined a man would look at the woman he loved. Damn. They really do love each other more than anything in the world.

I try to stop my shoulders from hunching. The action gives away too much information on my feelings. Ever since the first kill this week, I've had trouble hiding them. I think I subconsciously knew the end of my vengeance was coming. My task nearly complete.

Bosco spots me and rises to his feet. It must have jostled my mother's hand because her eyes flit open and scan the room. They land on me. I hold my breath wondering what she will say. She holds out a hand to me. I don't move. Can't.

After a beat my mother drops her hand. "I'm sorry Elena. I hadn't meant it the way it sounded." She sounds sincere. I want to believe her. My walls are falling. I don't have the energy to fortify them.

"It's fine." I reply with a shrug.

"No it's not. You have always been my little warrior. I gave you a shitty childhood." She's not wrong. I give a little laugh.

"I had no complaints." It's true. I knew from an early age that there was a reason for everything my mother did. I never wanted to burden her with my frustrations.

"You're right. You didn't. You went along with everything I did. Never complained when I had you pack up your toys in the middle of the night, or run into the woods when our car was run off the road." Those are just a small smattering of our obstacles.

"Would it have done any good?" I ask. My mother smiles.

"It wasn't the life I wanted for you." I finally shuffle closer. Enough so she can grab my hand. I don't yet squeeze it back.

"Nor I." Says Bosco.

"Well it was the one I had, the one forced on me, but don't forget you suffered too. You may be blinded by a childhood love. I'm not. That man who you cling to so fiercely, he caused this. He could have prevented it, stopped it, ended it. He didn't." I press a finger to my chest for emphasis. "I did." Her eyes scan around the room. "I found the traitor in his family. I found the rapist. I found the rats. Me. The daughter he never knew existed. Born of the wife never good enough for his family. So forgive me if I am not so quick to bend the knee."

"Elena." My father says my name as he rounds the bed to stand next to me. I feel Luca's presence nearby. My head is a mess. I need to make a decision regarding him. For now he is offering his strength. I take it. He clasps his hand to mine and entwines our fingers. He doesn't say a word. Luca's letting me do this my way just as he said he would. I breathe in his silent support and let it wash over me.

"Don't." I say as I hold a hand up to Bosco. "I may carry your blood and by familia law need to marry and produce an heir, but I don't need to call you father to do it. I don't need to like you. Hell I don't even need to respect you. In a matter of weeks Luca and I will marry and together we will usher in a new era. One where the females are not seen as weak. They are not just breeders or toys for you men." I look around the room. "Many of you don't know me. But I know each and every one of you. I know your dirty secrets. This is the only warning you will get. Clean up your act, or get out."

Luca pipes in to finish my warning. "Because once we say I do. We'll be coming for you." I hadn't wanted him to speak. I'm glad he did. He knew before I did that I needed him to help show a united front to the leaders of this family. We turn to leave the room as it erupts in protest.

The men don't know what I know about them. With a smile I turn back to them. "From my research, only two of you are true assholes and deserving of punishment. I'll let you figure out amongst yourselves who they are. One of you beats his wife. Sent her to the hospital twice this year already and covered it up. The other is skimming from the men under him. Keeping the hard working soldiers below him groveling for scraps."

With a smile, I grab Luca's hand again. "Let them stew and sweat it out." I whisper to him before the sound of one of the men rustling for his side piece hits my ears. I retrieve my knife from my pocket as Luca grabs his gun. While I have mine raised as a threat. Luca pulls the trigger.

The Capo of the fifth district falls. Blood running from his knee. Gino. "Elena gave her warning. This is mine. Do not cross us." I give Luca's hand a squeeze before releasing it. I walk over to Gino. Using my knife, I tip his chin up. "Hit your wife Sarah again and I will personally chop off your cock, stuff it up your ass and leave you on your father's grave to bleed out. Am I understood?" His eyes stare daggers at me. Whatever his thoughts are, I want to assure him mine are far my gruesome and painful. While his moves for retribution will undoubtedly fall flat. Mine won't.

With a steady hand, my knife travels along his jaw and across his cheek. I press with just enough pressure for the top few layers of skin to break and blood to lightly drip to coat my blade.

Luca speaks. "She asked you a question."

Hmm...maybe having someone to trust and have my back wouldn't be so bad. I'm not there yet. I'm still not ready for the last of my walls to fall. If anyone will be successful, it will be Luca.

Do I want that?

"Yes, I understand." Gino replies through clenched teeth.

"Good." I smile kindly at him, though it is anything but. Then I tap him with the flat side of the blade on the cheek before walking away.

Together Luca and I walk to the stairs. Before we ascend them. I give my mom the peace offering I can see she is hoping for. "I love you mom. Get some rest." The tension from my mother's face and shoulders instantly drops. So does Bosco's.

Luca squeezes my waiting hand and together we walk out of the basement.

CHAPTER TWENTY-ONE

Elena

Luca doesn't say a word as he leads me upstairs to our room. Yep our room. I was officially moving in with him. His decision. He wants to get to know me. His future wife.

We had a long talk on the drive back. He swears he doesn't want to trap me here. I will need to make some concessions with him. They are meant for my protection. I told him as long as we communicate about them and if his demands are unreasonable than I have the ability to negotiate.

Entering the room, I avoid looking at the bed. My body has been boiling with need since Luca wrapped his hand over mine and pointed it at my final hit-man. In my heart I know I can trust him. My brain is still hesitant. And my damn libido is a horny bitch. I waited too damn long to have sex and now she is rebelling against me, I swear. Just looking at Luca and I get wet and my mouth pools with the desire to lick him.

The door clicks shut behind us. I hear the lock snap into place. I can feel the desire to panic begin to rise. Everything I have been mentally holding back is crashing in on me. My desire for revenge never let me process things fully. I pushed emotions away, held back truths from even myself. Now I have nothing left to hide behind. The reasons mom and I ran are gone and the Caruso men have the Cartel on the run.

Which means I don't have to.

So why do I feel so empty? I should be overjoyed that my list is nearly complete.

Luca is in the room with me. I can't let him see me break down. He's already said he's not letting me out of his sight. He assured me I could cry, scream, rage, whatever I needed and he would stand beside me. My damn traitorous heart had skipped a beat at his words.

Working hard to put my once every day mask back on my face, I turn to Luca. "I'm going to take a shower." I take a step to him, and kiss him on the cheek. What I really want to do is throw myself at him and let him have his way with me.

It feels like it takes forever for my feet to carry me to the bathroom. The moment the door is closed and locked behind me, the mask falls away.

I knew I had taken it a step too far. The kiss was out of character. I could see the wheels turning in Luca's head after I did it. I just prayed that Luca would give me the space I need right now.

Stepping into the shower without bothering to strip, I let the water soak my clothes. The water joining my tears as I allow myself to break. My knees give out and I fall to the shower floor.

Vengeance has been paid to those that chased my mom and me. The final hit-man contracted by Santo is dead. The Uncle that chased my mother off while pregnant had suffered and died. My mother was happy. Really happy, and she got her kidney and was recovering.

So why didn't I feel relieved?

This was the moment I had worked towards for years. Is it because I didn't get retribution against my father? I wanted him to pay. I wanted him to know a fraction of my suffering. Knowing how in love my mother still was with him, I knew I couldn't act. Any pain to him, would hurt my mother. I couldn't do it. The tears crashed down harder. My body shakes from my sobbing. Mixed with my adrenaline crash, I'm not sure I will be able to pick myself up off the floor after this.

Thoughts of the future flit around in my head. None lasting more than a few moment. None except one. Maybe after the wedding I will feel better. Maybe after Bosco is no longer Don I can feel at ease. Luca and I would be taking most of the power from him. It wouldn't be done underhandedly like I wanted, but it still can have the desired effect.

Over the rushing of the water I hear someone knocking on the door and a muffled call of my name. Even without being able to hear them clearly, I know it is Luca speaking.

I don't have the energy to answer. Don't want to answer. I want the calm of darkness to take me. The last reserves of my adrenaline are gone, my emotions shot.

Vengeance had been served yet I feel so empty.

CHAPTER TWENTY-TWO

Luca

I couldn't stand it any longer. The sound of her cries was like a knife to the heart. She knew she was going to break once she walked into that bathroom. I knew it too, yet I held onto the hope that she would accept my offer to help. I couldn't take her pain away. As much as I wanted to, the damage was already done.

Strolling over to my desk I begin ripping open the drawers, searching for my lock picking tools. I could kick the door down. I want to. It isn't reinforced like the doors that lead to the hallways. Kicking something would release some of the pent up frustration I am feeling. My body is thrumming with energy and no place to aim it.

Sensing Elena's pain and vulnerability through the door, I know I can't act like a caveman and storm in there. She has been so strong. I knew she was bound to break.

A few moments with the tools in the lock and I feel the distinctive click of it mechanism. Slowly I enter the room. Knowing I would see her crying, and witnessing her small curled frame on the shower floor had me wanting to raise every last fucker that ever messed with her and kill them again. It wouldn't be a gunshot to the head. I would peel their skin back one layer at a time. Let them slowly bleed out until they had no pain left to feel. Only then would I send them back to hell.

Elena is amazing. The very definition of strength, grit, and determination. Not to mention her brilliance and beauty. It isn't an appropriate time, but my dick hardens.

Not now. As much as I desired her, my cock isn't going to help the situation. I need to be there for her emotionally.

Elena is the first person I want to be the rock for. Raised in the mafia I was taught to be a hard man, dominant, controlling, and decisive. Rule with an iron fist in the office and at home. The women in my life, aside from my mother and nanny growing up were used for release and then released. I got off and they got out. I was never rude or mean. I was direct and told the ladies up front. I had my share of women that thought they could claim me. That somehow they could get me to cuddle or call them back for a second night.

It didn't happen. Not until Elena. I want to wrap her up in my arms every chance I get. I want her in my bed every night. Mornings too. Fuck. I really do love her. Strange. A few weeks ago I thought I would be marrying Milan in three years. Now I am marrying Elena in a week. Damn.

And here I am breaking into my bathroom listening to the sobs of the strongest woman I have ever met and it is breaking my heart. I knew she needed to cry. It would be therapeutic for her.

Didn't mean I didn't want to hold her as she processed everything. Her life has been nothing but chaos. Running, hiding, fighting. My Psycho Princess deserved a break. She needed one. She needed someone she could trust. Someone she could lean on. I would be that someone. I won't give her a choice.

The thought of her seeking solace in anyone else's arm causes me to growl under my breath as I slowly enter the shower. Never. She is mine. She may not love me, but she will. We have the foundation laid. The events of the last twenty-four hours have cemented our presence in each other's lives. I have shown her that she can trust me. That I won't bulldoze her wishes. I won't let her run without me. And I won't undermine her authority. I showed my trust in her.

Seeing her curled in the shower still in her clothes shatters me. Kneeling before her, I reach out but don't touch her. "Baby girl..." She lets out a huge sob. Her body shakes vigorously.

That's it. I can't wait for her to come to me. I pick her up and put her in my lap. Clothes still on, I press my back against the wall. Water soaks me in a matter of seconds. She cries harder as she turns in my lap. Her knees fall to either side of my hips. I drag her body closer. Chest to chest she continues to cry as I rub circles down her back. "I've got you sweetheart. I won't ever let you go." She grips me tighter. I put my head in her neck and breath her in then place a chaste kiss to her skin.

I'm not sure how long we sit there. It was long enough for the water to run cold. I reach up with one hand and turn the water off. Without a word spoken Elena chokes back her next sob and makes to stand. I can't let her go yet, so I grab her tighter. "Not yet. Let me hold you."

She shakes her head at me. "I'm okay now."

She tries to move again. I hold her tighter. "No you're not, and that's okay."

"I said I am good!" She says with more force. Her feet kick out. They slip on the wet tile as she tries to get enough traction to stand. Not happening.

I curl my fingers into her hair and force her head back. I needed her attention. "No. You're not. You have been bottling things up for far too long. I get that you needed to. Not saying it was a bad thing. You had a lot on your shoulders. A lot of shit tossed at you. And you tackled it all like the warrior princess you are."

"I thought I was a Psycho Princess?" She teases lightly. The faint ghost of a smile skims the corner of her lip.

"You are. You are my Psycho Princess." I kiss her nose. I need her to see as well as feel my sincerity. "That doesn't mean you are invincible. In here..." I use a finger to mimic circling the room. "...When it's just the two of us. You can let it out. You can show me the cracks in your armor. I might not be able to patch you up, but I damn well will hold you through it. I get you haven't had anyone to lean on aside from your mom for far too long. I'm here now. I'm not going anywhere. Lean on me. Cry on me. Fight me if you need to. And know that you aren't alone anymore."

Taking me by surprise, she smashes her lips into mine.

That's not where I intended the conversation to go. The thought slips my mind as her tongue breaches my lips and begins to explore my mouth. With her still clinging to me, I manage to get to my feet. Her hands claw at my clothing. It makes me smile against her lips.

For someone whose sexual experience is limited, she is getting bold and I love it. Our conversation wasn't done. Not by a long shot. I'd let her have this moment first.

Her fingers tear at my clothing. First my shirt is torn from my chest. Next her hands are unbuttoning my pants and ripping them down my thighs.

Once I am naked I assist her in removing her clothes as well. Fuck. She is beautiful. Curvy in all the right places. Firm perky tits and an ass I wanted to slap then worship. She is a bit too skinny still for someone her height. We will work on that together. She no longer needs to worry about money or being too busy running to care for herself properly. I will see to it that her every need, her every desire is met. As long as it involves me.

She climbs back into my arms. Her naked body rubbing against my hard as steel cock. My mind is telling me to stop. She isn't ready for this. Not truly. She will regret it in the morning when she is thinking straight again.

My dick is telling my brain to shut up. I am dripping pre-cum. I want, no need to bury myself in her. I think she feels it to. She feels the connection between us and needs more. I need in her.

I grab her ass to support her as I start walking. Her legs wrap around me and she attacks my neck with kisses. Moving quickly. I exit the bathroom, cross the bedroom and toss her on the bed.

Shit. I can't fuck her without knowing she won't regret it. I worked too damn hard to build her trust. I want her. If I sense any doubt I won't make a move. If we start and I feel her hesitate I will stop.

I see only hunger in her eyes as she stares up at me. Damn she looks like an angel. Her hair spread across my pillow. Her lips swollen from our kissing. I've never had a more beautiful woman in my arms. And she is naked, in my bed, looking at me like I am the best damn treat she is ever going to devour.

"Are you sure about this?" I ask. She nods. It isn't good enough. I need the words. I need to hear the conviction in her voice. "I don't want you to regret this. If you are looking for release I will give it to you in other ways. We don't need to have sex for me to pleasure you."

Her eyes soften as they connect with mine. The hunger is there still. Only now it is mixed with trust. She trusts me. Damn, I can feel my chest puffing up. I feel ten foot tall. "I want you Luca. All of you. I won't regret it." She gets to her knees and crawls to the end of the bed. Her arms wrap around my neck. "I have spent years trying to get over my crush on you. Trying to deny I felt anything for you as I watched you through my computer screen. Nothing I did worked. You embedded yourself here." She grabs my hand and places it over her heart. I feel it beating in time with mine. "I have been running my entire life. I'm done. No more. You said you would chase me." Keeping my hand on her chest, she wraps her arms around my neck and pulls me in for a kiss. "I don't want you to chase me. I'm coming to you. Take me. Make me yours."

Hell fucking yes! "You're mine." I push her back onto the bed. My body on top of hers, I keep the bulk of the weight off with my elbows anchored on the bed.

"I'm yours." She smiles and kisses me again.

I skim kisses down her jaw then neck. Working my way down her body. She's a virgin. She is going to be tight as hell and I cannot wait to feel her squeezing my cock. I don't want to hurt her. There will be pain I won't be able to avoid. I'll lessen it by making sure she is ready for me.

She's panting heavily. Her eyes never leaving mine as I move down her body and between her legs. I look to make sure she is still with me. That there is no hesitation in her face.

There isn't. She licks her lips in anticipation as I lower my mouth to her thigh. I kiss the left one first. Moving closer to the promise land, I kiss the innermost part of her right thigh.

Her folds are glistening wet. "Fuck babe. I can't wait to taste you." My voice is huskier than it's ever been. I don't think I have ever felt this much desire. Certainly never wanted to go down on a woman so bad. It's been years since I have. The women I have been with in the past have been dripping wet for me before I even touched them. I didn't need to go down on them to get them ready. Nor did I want to. So I didn't.

I haven't even tasted her yet and I know I won't be able to get enough.

I feel her legs tense. They begin to close around my shoulders. Nope. Can't have that. I tear my gaze away from her pussy. Her hands are hiding her breasts. Her eyes are on the ceiling. She's pulling away from me. I don't want that. I want her to like, no love, everything that I do to her. "Elena."

"Yeah." She whispers. Her voice is shaky.

"I can st..." I don't even finish the word before she is sitting bolt upright.

"No." She practically screams the word. "Sorry." She shakes her head at me. "I want this. I want you. I'm just nervous. When I said virgin, I mean everything. I haven't done any of this with anyone. I haven't even watched porn. I have no idea what to do with my hands. Where are my eyes supposed to be? Are you expecting me to talk during it?" She's rambling. It's fucking adorable.

I sit up so I am eye level with her. "I love that you are completely untouched. I would have to murder any man that came before me. And there will be no man after me." She nods her head in agreement. "There is no right or wrong thing to do with your hands. Do whatever feels natural. Whatever feels good. But I want your eyes on me. I want you to know who is giving you pleasure and I want to watch as you come undone by my tongue." Her tongue pokes out and licks her lips. I take over for her and kiss and lick them. "If you want to talk during it, go ahead. I will have you screaming my name as you cum."

"Luca." She ducks her head and hides in my chest.

"Babe. Nothing to be ashamed about. If you don't like something, tell me. Want more of something, moan for me and I'll give it to you. You want to ask questions, I'll answer every god damn one. It's just us in here. You and me."

The smile that lights up her face almost has me cumming on the bedsheets. Shit. I really need to get inside of her soon or I'm not going to last more than a couple of thrusts. I give her another kiss that I deepen until she's moaning. When I go to pull back, she grunts her disapproval and rocks her hips against me.

Giving into her need. I keep kissing her. My right hand slides down her stomach and cups her pussy. Shit. She is dripping wet. I slide a single finger through her folds and bring it to my mouth. I pull away from her long enough to lick my finger clean. I can't help but to let out a moan of my own. Fuck she tastes good. I need more. I give her another quick kiss and lower her back to the bed.

She thrusts her hips again. Her pussy rubbing along my erection. "Not yet Elena."

"Please." She whimpers in-between kisses as she continues to rock against me.

"Soon." I say as I kiss down her chest again. My teeth grazing a nipple before sucking it into my mouth.

Looking back up at her face. I see the pout on her lips. Her hips struggle against my body. I'm keeping her pinned in place. "Nope. None of that." I give an extra hard bite to her breast. Her eyes flick to mine. Staring daggers at me. "I'm not rushing this. I am going to worship your body and you are going to take everything I give you." I latch onto her other nipple and lave it with kisses. "Okay?"

"Yes." She moans as I give one last suckle before releasing with a pop. I work my way back down her body. I can't wait any longer. I spread her folds and run my tongue along her whole slit. I circle her clit without touching it. She squirms underneath me. I wrap my arms around her thighs and pull her tighter to me. She isn't going anywhere until I feel her cum.

I tease her for another minute before I give in. I bite and suck until she is a moaning mess. Bringing my eyes up to hers I keep her gaze locked on as I slip a finger into her entrance. Fuck she is tight.

Her legs are shaking. It doesn't take me long to push her over the edge. Her orgasm crashing over her. Her eyes break from mine as they roll back. Her legs spasm around my head. I fucking love it. I continue to stroke her with my tongue and finger until the last wave of her orgasm fades.

She lays limp as I crawl up her body. Her eyes come back into focus as I settle my cock at her entrance. "Again please!"

I laugh. Only my Psycho Princess could have me laughing with my hard cock pressed against her. "I'll give you as many as you want baby girl. But the next one will be with you wrapped around my cock." I press in a few inches. Making sure to go slow and not hurt her more than necessary. She is tighter than any woman I have ever been with. Shit. I don't even recall if I have ever been with a virgin before.

The tip of my cock hits her maidenhood. I use one hand to rub at her clit. My mouth envelops hers. I overwhelm her with as much pleasure as I can. She's moaning into my mouth as I thrust forward. Burying my cock all the way in her. Her moan turns to a scream that I swallow as I continue to kiss her through the pain.

I don't move. The walls of her pussy are clenched down

tight around me. I pull back from her lips and dip my head to her shoulder. My breathing is heavy. I am two second from cumming. Her pussy feels too good. I can't. Not yet. I need her to cum with me.

We stay still in each other's arms for several long minutes. I can tell her pain is fading when she hesitantly moves her hips. It's a small motion. She doesn't gasp in pain or stop suddenly. I take it as my cue to move. I pull out of her slowly and rock back in.

Her legs wrap around my hips. Her heels dig into my ass. She's ready. I thrust again, hard this time. I increase my pace. Fighting to keep control of myself, I keep my eyes locked on hers. The pain is gone. She's completely in the moment with me. I want to tell her I love her. That I'll worship her body every day. She's it for me. I don't need anyone else in my life. She is the Queen I always wanted but never thought I'd get.

We lose ourselves to passion. My thrusts going out of control. I'm a man on a mission. I need her to cum again. I want to feel her pussy clench down on me as she screams out my name.

"Luca. Fuck, Luca." I love that she's found her voice. I want to hear more of it.

Keeping my dick buried in her, I pull her to my chest as I sit back on my heels. I'm deeper in her in this position. Her hands claw at my back as I bounce her up and down. "So deep. Holy shit." She's barely coherent. Her pussy begins to flutter. Her eyes roll back in her head as her orgasm peaks again. "LUCA!" She screams. Her nails drawing blood from my back.

I continue to thrust into her. One, two, three more times before I'm roaring my own release. I pull her with me as I fall backwards onto the bed. My cock is softening inside her. I don't want to pull out. I want to stay in her forever.

Her head rests on my chest. Neither of us able to move. I stroke her hair and stare down at her. This beautiful woman is all mine. Every night I will be inside her seeking a repeat performance of this. She better be ready for me. I won't be stopping until she is swollen with my kid. Even after. I won't ever tire of her body or her fire. I want all that she has to give me.

She rubs her cheek against my chest. I use a finger under her chin to tilt her head up to look at me. She has tears in her eyes. Fuck. "Babe. Talk to me." She tries to pull away from me. Nope not happening. I won't have her regretting this. She was ready. There was no doubt in my mind. I won't let her start putting it there by second guessing a damn thing we just did. "What's wrong? Did I hurt you?"

"I'm fine." Elena says softly. The tears now dripping down her face. Fuck. The universal word for woman that means they are anything but fine. I give her a stern look. She must sense that I don't believe her as she tries to argue. "It's true. I am fine."

"I'm going to need more than that. You're crying. That means you aren't fine." I sit up and pull her with me. We are face to face. My arms snaked around her waist holding her firmly.

She sighs and shakes her head. "I don't feel anything. I'm no longer mad or angry. I got what I wanted. I killed the man hunting me. I made the man who ruined my mom's life and subsequently mine pay, and I put the fear of god into the Capos of the family. I did what I sought to do and now I've had mind blowing sex with you."

"Mind blowing huh?" I can't help but tease her. My ego has doubled in size. "You don't sound fine. Do you regret what we just did?"

"Fuck no." She looks like I slapped her.

"Sorry babe. I had to ask. When I saw the tears I feared you regretted it. Regretted me."

She slams her lips to mine. Shit. My lips are going to be bruised tomorrow. Her arms go around my neck and hold me close. Her tongue dances against mine for a moment before she pulls back and rests her forehead against mine. "I don't regret it. I don't regret you. I love you." My breathing stalls. "I know it's probably too soon for me to say it, but you wanted me to talk. This is me talking. I've loved you since the first time I watched you on camera. You were trying to escape Milan and Ravinia. They had you cornered in the kitchen the night before the Council's Gala. Milan wasn't invited. She was too young. Ravinia was trying to get you to take her anyway. You were so sweet when you tried to let her down easy. I could see how frustrated and pissed you were but you didn't take it out on her." She rests her head against my chest. She loves me. Holy shit.

"Elena." I need to tell her how I feel.

"No. Don't say it back. I don't want you to say it because you feel obligated to." She tries to get out of my grip. Her hands push against my chest.

"Elena look at me." She doesn't. She does stop her moving. Except to put her arms up to cover her breasts. She is feeling vulnerable. I can feel her walls going up but I won't relent. I cup her cheeks. She won't make eye contact with me. I talk anyway because I know she is listening. "I don't say shit I don't mean. I won't ever lie to you. When I say I love you, believe it. Because I do. I fucking love you Elena. I wanted to say it when I was buried inside you. I wanted to say it the day you climbed into my lap and shot at the car that hit us. I love you." I had to repeat it in the hopes she absorbs my words.

Her hands drop and she's back hugging and kissing me.

"I love you Luca. I'm sorry you thought I regretted having sex with you. I don't. How could anyone regret that? It was amazing. It was nothing like I thought it would be, but it was everything I could have dreamed it would be. I wasn't lying when I said I was fine. I'm not used to sharing my feelings with anyone."

"Try for me."

She nods. "After we were done. My mind went off on its own. I couldn't control where the thoughts went. I was swimming in bliss until I realized I was happy because of you. Not because of my vengeance. It confused and overwhelmed me. I haven't been happy in so long. I thought I'd be happy or at the least relieved when I was done. I wasn't. I was empty. You filled that in me. Emotionally and physically. I've never felt a connection to anyone like I do with you. It scared me for a moment. You hold my heart in your hands and you could break it at any moment. I've gotten through a lot of shit in my life, but I won't be able to come back from that. Please don't break me."

"Never." I kiss her with every ounce of my soul. "I will never break your heart. You are too damn precious to me. You are my everything now. You are going to be my wife. My Queen. I love you Elena. I will always love you."

"I love you too Luca."

I need more than those three words to reassure her. "You are fucking amazing. I want to give you everything I can, so long as you let me go along for the ride. I want you to not have to lean on me, but choose to, and if a moment comes when you need me, I'll be there. If you want sex for pleasure I'm always down for that. You need to work out a frustration and want some hate sex. I'm your guy. As long as you don't actually hate me." I kiss her nose. "You're feeling lost and need my arms around you, I will always hold you. Which is what I think you need right now." I snuggle her in closer to me as I lay us down on the bed. I move her so she is laying on top of me. "You need to feel that I'm not leaving you. And I need you to trust me." I kiss her forehead. She sighs and rests her head against me.

"I trust you." She says it quickly. Not a moment of hesitation. "I didn't think I would, at least not this fast. I didn't want to. Trusting people isn't something I have ever done. Even Ronan who is the closest thing I've had to a father figure, I still held at arm's length. It's been my default setting for so long I didn't think I could live any other way."

"But now you do?"

"With you. Yes." Elena replies as she kissed my chest and snuggles deeper into my arms. "You ran after me when I didn't think I wanted you to. You handed me the gun when I wondered if you'd put a bullet in my hit-man's head. And you held my hand and let me lead in front of the Capos. You let me be who I needed to be and lent me your strength even when I didn't need it. Or even want it." A chuckle from deep in my chest rocks us both as she continues. "You are stubborn in all the best ways. I don't feel judged by you. I don't feel pitied. And I don't feel crazy. I've never had someone like that. It's something I didn't know I needed. So yes. I trust you. I want to marry you."

"Good. Because if you didn't show up next weekend. I would hunt you down and drag you down the aisle." She sits up and straddles my hips. My cock is hard again.

"Are we done talking now?" Her ass is pressed against my cock. I wasn't sure she would want to take me again tonight. I thought she might be too sore.

"Yeah, we're done." I say as her hips begin to rock. Yep. She's ready for round two. I pull her down to me and roll us so she is under me. Fuck she's gorgeous when she is flush with desire. Her cheeks are red. Her chest rising quickly. I rise to my knees so I can get a good look at her body.

Her arms reach out for me. I'm just out of reach. "Please fuck me." She says as she wiggles her hips and grabs her breasts with both hands.

"No." I reply with a small shake of my head. Confusion and a bit of hurt flash in her eyes. "I'm not fucking you tonight. I'm going to make love to you."

The most brilliant smile I have ever seen spread across her face as I lean down to devour her for the second, third, and fourth time of the night.

CHAPTER TWENTY-THREE

Elena

The next day we were awoken by the sound of people arguing. Luca immediately lunges for the nightstand and grabs his gun. I can't help but smile. "Relax. It's Ravinia." I know we have nothing to fear within the walls of the compound. Even without the guards stationed all around. I have made several advancements to the security system. We would be alerted well before there was an intruder. Well, at least an intruder that was genuinely dangerous. Ravinia was only dangerous to Bosco's bank account.

"Ugh, what does she want?" He grumbles as he rolls out of bed. I quickly follow. He is pulling on his pants as I pull on my shirt. "What does she always want? Money."

"Fuck. I thought we were done with her." We're both dressed now and moving to the door. Luca opens it allows me to go first.

"I don't think we ever will be. Milan is still her daughter." I remind him.

Milan has been living at the mansion with us. True to

Bosco's word, nothing in their relationship has changed. If anything they have gotten closer. Same with her and her biological dad Mario. It's funny watching them now. I had observed Mario spoiling her with kindness while still being professional. Now the lines are blurred. He is still her guard and more vigilant than ever. Only now they greet each other openly with hugs and a kiss on the cheek. It warms my heart. I'm still slightly bitter and reluctant to build a relationship with Bosco. I know I need to work on it. I see the suffering in his eyes when I enter a room he is in. I see the longing in his eye when I hug mom but not him.

Luca pulls me out of my thoughts. "Shit with everything else going on. I forgot about the whole Ravinia and Mario thing." We pick up speed as we get closer to the stairs and the yelling gets louder. "I should get down there," he says.

The commotion has drawn people from all over the house. I can't help but to cringe as I notice how many Capos are at the house. I think it's all of them. "Fuck," grumbles Luca as his eyes land on members of the council. They came early to have meetings and discussions before our wedding this weekend.

My sentiments exactly. "Fuck." If Milan's parentage is revealed to them, it could destroy her. Bosco too. She isn't his biological daughter, but he did raise her. He loves her. Milan is standing off to the side. Mario looks uncomfortable. I can tell he wants to pull Milan into his arms and comfort her. He won't. He is too professional and knows his place. He won't risk exposing them.

"Enough Ravinia!" Shouts Bosco. "You are only embarrassing yourself."

"Me?" She hollers back. Her face is red, her hair a mess. Even her normally pressed to perfection outfit is wrinkled. "I'm embarrassing? Says the man who married me when he already had a wife." Bosco runs his hand over his face. He knows this conversation is already out of hand. It's too late to stop it. "You lied to me. You lied to the families!"

She's trying to rally the Capos. A quick scan of the room would show her that she isn't winning anyone over. "Technically I never lied." Rebuts Bosco. "The Council knew I had married Violet. It had been approved. And at the time of our marriage I was to assume I was a widow."

"Assumed but didn't know for sure." Her voice is cracking the more she screams.

"That's argumentative and besides the point." Bosco is standing alongside the Council. He takes a few steps closer to Ravinia who is centered in the Foyer. "I was married before I was Don. Before I met you. She was declared dead. My father's Consigliere confirmed it. Due to that lie, I believed I was not still married when I married you."

"You mean the Consigliere that ran that bitch off." Ravinia is grasping at straws. The Council has already agreed that Violet's marriage to Bosco is still legal and therefore his marriage to Ravinia is not.

"Watch your mouth!" Bosco growls back. I've seen him angry. I've never seen him like this though. "And yes. That one. The same one that the Council voted in and backed for the last thirty years. Not one of them suspected his treachery. Even I failed at that." His eyes soften as he turns to me. "Elena was the one to learn the truth."

"You mean your bastard daughter?" Her words sting.

"I'm not a bastard." I shout. I hadn't meant to talk. Her hateful word stung even if they weren't true.

Ravinia glares at me. Her eyes daring me to speak again. Oh, I so want to. Bosco beats me too it. "Since Violet isn't dead, our marriage is still very much intact. So, you're wrong. Elena is not a bastard. She is my daughter. My eldest. My heir."

"No! I'm your wife." Tears of frustration run down her cheeks as she continues to try to argue. If she wasn't such a bitch I would feel sorry for her.

"I'm sorry Ravinia. It was never legal." Bosco's voice softens. It sounds like he doesn't want to yell anymore. He wants her to concede she is wrong. Accept that there was no love between them and move on.

"No." Ravinia shakes her head as she continues not to believe him. "She wasn't strong enough to be your wife. I am. It's why I was chosen. The Council chose me."

"No. My father chose. I never wanted to marry again. Violet was my heart and soul. The only wife I ever wanted." He pauses and takes another step towards Ravinia. "While I didn't love you. I did care for you. And I love our daughter Milan."

"Ha." She barks a laugh. "Your daughter?" Oh fuck. Those of us around the room that know the truth instantly tense. She can't be dumb enough to reveal the truth. She would be throwing herself under the boss. She can't be that stupid can she? "She's not yours." Fuck. Yes she is. "You weren't man enough to get me pregnant."

Milan gasps. Mario grabs her. Holding her in a hug and shielding her from the eyes of the Capos and Council members that didn't know. "Ravinia, don't." Warns Bosco.

"The truth is out Bosco. You, the great Don couldn't produce an heir so I had to fake one. What does the family think of you now? Who will sit on your throne now?" Bosco didn't respond to her. He was too busy looking at Milan who stared at her mom in horror. They may not have had the best relationship but Elena could tell Milan tried to please her mother. She was begging for affection and approval from her.

"You're shooting blanks old man, who's to say Elena is

even your daughter. Maybe that whore lied to you." Ravinia continues her rant as the Council begins to whisper.

"My mother is not a whore." I retort as I stomp towards her. I want to slap her, stab her, and shoot her all at once. Luca's arm grasps me around the middle and stops me.

Bosco joins the two of us at my side. Milan and Mario behind him, they are flanked by Massimo, Val and Ricco. "Elena is my daughter. Three separate DNA tests have confirmed it. The Council has already received those reports. She is my heir." I've calmed down enough that Luca has released me. His left hand holds my right. Shoulder to shoulder he is my strength. My reason to remain calm. Bosco takes another step closer to me and grabs my free hand. "Elena will be marrying Luca this Saturday. It's why the Council is here.

The Capos all start to grumble amongst themselves. They weren't in the know yet. Today was supposed to be the announcement. "A wedding?" One man asks.

"Yes." Replies Bosco. "Luca to Elena. She is my heir and has agreed to the union."

"Milan is not your daughter?" Asks another Capo.

The room is silent. Even Ravinia is quiet. "She is my daughter." Milan steps up to him and takes her place by his other side. She chances a glance at me. I make sure to give her a big smile and nod. I want her to know I have her back. She and I don't have a relationship. Not yet anyway. I hope someday we do. Maybe today can be the start. "My blood does not run through her veins, but she is every bit still my daughter. If I hear one word against her. I will cut out that man's tongue. Am I understood?"

Tears form in Milan's eyes as she moves closer to Bosco. Mario is right behind her. Pride is glistening in his eyes for Bosco.

A chorus of "Yes Don." Echo around the room.

Bosco nods his approval before turning back to his ex-wife. "Ravinia. You have caused enough trouble. I tried to do right by you. I gave you companionship when I couldn't give you love. I bought you everything your heart desired and treated you like gold yet still nothing was good enough for you. Never did you stand proudly at my side. Never did you speak up when someone spoke against me. You may have been my wife in name, but you were never my Queen. Violet understood the role as you never did. She would have backed me as a Don's wife should. As I know Elena will do with Luca."

Ravinia begins to scream again. She's shouting profanities and lies. "Enough!" Comes a familiar voice from the corner. It's my mom. She is still pale and recovering from her surgery. She takes two steps into the circle. Guards and Capos parting so she can join us. "Guard." She speaks calmly though it is dripping with authority.

Two men step up. Massimo and Paolo.

An overwhelming amount of pride is pouring off of Bosco. My mom didn't need to get out of bed for this. Bosco could have handled it just fine. Being the Queen she is. My mother knew better. She would stand by his side even on her deathbed. Which thanks to the new Kidney, she is no longer laying on.

Bosco leaves his eyes on my mom as he speaks again to Ravinia. "Ravinia, when I learned of Violet's survival I tried to do right by you. I gave you a penthouse, filled a bank account for you, and armed you with a team of guards to keep you safe. I asked nothing of you. And yet you came here today and pissed all over my generosity."

Massimo and Paolo have Ravinia by the arms. She is tugging against their hold while still trying to slander my family. Massimo clamps his hand over her mouth. I smile at him and I feel Luca chuckle next to me. Massimo looks to us and gives a wink. "Out of respect for your time as my wife and for Milan. I will not excommunicate you." Ravinia seems to sag in relief. It's hard to tell since she is being held up. "But you are banished from this city and from this country. You will be sent to Sicily where the families of old will keep watch on you. I suggest you accept your place there quickly. You will have no title and no sway over the Council."

She screeches as Massimo and Paolo drag her from the room.

Bosco turns away from the door they left through and addresses the room. "Men, I need to speak to my daughters. Please grab a coffee, our meeting will resume shortly." The men leave and Bosco leads our group into the library.

Bosco pulls Milan into a hug the moment the door closes behind us. "I'm so sorry Milan. I didn't want to believe she would cause a scene like that."

"I know." She nods and replies softly.

"I never wanted you to go through that. I know you love your mother but she is a vile evil woman when she wants to be. And it seems that is happening more and more often."

Milan nods. "Yeah. I've felt it for a while. I thought maybe I was doing something wrong."

"Never." Say Bosco and Mario together.

Bosco gives a nod to Mario. Allowing him to take Milan into his arms and speak to her. "You did nothing wrong. Your mother has always pushed you to be someone you aren't. We should have never let that happen."

Milan nods. "So what happens now? If mom is going to Sicily."

"You are staying here. We will fly you to visit your mother whenever you wish." Bosco says reassuring her.

Now it's my turn to reassure her. "Your place is here. With us."

Milan turns to Luca and I with tears in her eyes. "Really?"

"Absolutely." Luca says in agreement as he gives my hand a squeeze.

CHAPTER TWENTY-FOUR

Elena

It is the night before my wedding. It isn't going to be a big glamorous affair. It's not my style. Thankfully it's not Luca's either. I wasn't like other girls growing up. I never imagined my wedding day. Never thought I would settle down long enough to find someone, let alone trust them enough to marry them.

We are at our rehearsal dinner. We rented out one of the Family's Italian Bistros. There are maybe fifty people here. I would have preferred less. The Council superseded our wishes. Luca convinced me to cave. Saying we would have plenty of battles we would need to pick in the future, and including them in the dinner was a small price to pay.

I hate when he's right. No I don't. I love it. Being with him allows me to pass some of my worries to him to deal with. I am learning quickly that I don't need to be in control of everything. I don't need to have eyes on everyone.

The dinner is going well. My family is here. All the cousins I've never met are slowly warming to me as I am

176

them. They seemed a bit apprehensive about their new found connection to the Mafia. Bosco had to assure them that they've been linked this entire time. Ever since his first date with Mom, they were under his protection. Their tune changed after Bosco provided them specific scenarios he had intervened with them in the past.

Everyone from Luca's side, and by his side, I mean the Mafia men and families, appear to be behaving. There are no grumblings about Mom and I's sudden appearance, or the parentage of Milan. The last week was spent calming the storm and assuring everyone that the Caruso Family was strong and more powerful than ever.

The Council had me regale them with the tale of my revenge. Bosco was tense throughout it. The Mafia men prided themselves on keeping women and children out of the fighting. With me being in the middle of it, by my own design no less, I had pissed a few of the men off and damaged their egos. Once they learned my reasoning their trepidation eased away. They made me agree to keep out of the fighting in the future and let Luca lead. He had squeezed my hand under the table then. His touch reminding me of the private conversation we had already agreed to the night before as he made love to me.

As long as I wasn't pregnant or trying to jump in front of bullets. Luca would allow me to come with him on the less dangerous missions outside of the house. As Don they would be less than he was used to. Massimo would be stepping into his role as Underboss and those outings would now fall to him. Any enemy that came back alive was fair game for me to play with if I wanted to, or I could watch. I wasn't sure I still wanted blood on my hands. I had only done it to keep my mom and I safe. With the threat gone, and my list nearly complete I no longer felt the urge to defend or kill. The final plans to take the last name off was in place. It was time for me to find my peace.

Dad and Mom are seated to my right smiling and laughing. Yep. I'm calling him dad now. Our relationship is shaky at best. Point is, I'm trying. And as Luca likes to remind me. I have all the time in the world now since I'm never running again.

Or so he thinks. I like when he chases me. I might have to fake a run someday.

To Luca's left sits Massimo and Valentino. Milan was seated beside me but opted to move towards the guys while dessert was being brought out. She has been steadily finding herself. With her mom not hounding her every minute of the day, she has started to relax. Together, we even went shopping so she could teach me how to dress like a Mafia Queen, while I bought her her first pair of Converse Sneakers. She's finding her style is much more reserved and relaxed than the heels and dresses her mother forced on her.

Shopping was just the tip of the iceberg for Milan and I this week. After I showed my support at her staying and keeping her place in the family, the Council was forced to keep her title as the Don's second daughter.

After hours of talking and laughing while shopping I asked her to be my maid of honor. I didn't have many friends. Sadly Luna wouldn't be able to make an appearance but she promised to watch it live. Milan had thrown herself at me when I asked. She quickly said yes and inserted herself into the final wedding planning decisions with me. We had a ways to go to build our relationship. It would be worth it. I final had the makings of the family I never thought I'd have.

With Milan's hair both figuratively and literally down, the guys were much more open to her joining them in conversation. Val more than anyone. I think they shared common ground as part of the family while feeling like outsiders for being different. Val was the tech geek in an age when the Mafia was still very old school while Milan was the daughter of an over bearing mother who ruined her relationships before they could get started. Together they were learning to find their place. I'd like to think I was helping. I mean who better than the lost daughter of the Mafia Don who never had friends and didn't trust anyone.

I had trust now. I trusted Luca. I trusted my father. I even trusted the Council. We didn't always see eye to eye. That was fine with me. We could disagree from time to time, as long as everyone communicated their concerns and there was no back door wheeling and dealing. To ease my comfort I may or may not still be surveying them to be certain.

Now that Milan is no longer forced to mimic her mother, the guys have found out how smart she is. She also hates heels and hasn't worn a pair since. The minute she heard her mom's plane was in the air she threw every pair out her window and into the yard. Bosco and Mario were on the patio and laughed when they started raining down on them. She still likes dresses, but not short and tight. She likes flowing tea dresses or maxi dresses.

While I've been keeping Milan busy, I convinced Luca and the guys to redo Milan's room. Her mother had it decorated pink with flowers and doilies crowding every surface. When we got back the night of our shopping trip Milan was speechless. The walls were changed to a cream color with a single accent wall by her bed that was maroon. Turns out it's her favorite color and she hates pink and yellow. The white furniture was replaced with American Walnut. Floor to ceiling bookshelves were installed along the wall surrounding the window that now boasted a built in bench seat with an assortment of pillows.

Milan squealed and ran to the bench when she saw it. Then jumped on the bed before bouncing off and moving to her new desk. "I don't know what to say." She had said with visible tears in her eyes.

Bosco and Mario walked in at that moment. "It was long overdue." Admitted Bosco. "This room was never really yours. It was your mothers you just slept in it."

Milan laughed. "Yeah, she did that with everything."

"Not anymore." Said Mario. "This is your room. Don't like it. Change it. Want different furniture? I'll give you my credit card. Want to hang posters on every inch of all? Do it."

The tears then fell and ran heavily down her cheeks. "Your life is now your own. Enjoy it. Embrace it." Luca told her.

And here she was. Embracing the new her. Or rather the side of her she always had to hide. Dad stood and clinked his glass. The room quieted down. Speech time.

"First off I want to thank everyone for coming. For some of you the announcement came as a big surprise. In fact it did for all of us. Four weeks ago I never could have imagined my Violet coming back into my life, and I sure shit didn't picture her coming home with an adult daughter in tow." His gaze roves over to me. A large smile on his face and a twinkle in his eye. "My daughter. I wasn't part of her life for the first nineteen years. I'll be damned if I miss another moment." He pauses, then turns back to the guests. "As Don it was expected of me to have an heir. A male heir. While I wasn't blessed with that. I was blessed with something far greater. Two amazing daughters." I reached for Milan's hand. Neither of us caring that we were stretching over the three guys. We held hands tightly for a brief moment before I let go and brought my hand back to Luca. "Still, I needed an heir. Our family needs a strong leader at its helm. Years ago I found that in Luca. While not blood he is family." Everyone here knows Luca was once arranged to marry Milan. Dad doesn't name her as it is implied. I appreciate the detail to protect her from embarrassment though she has nothing to be embarrassed about. "With the return of my wife and Elena the plans were tweaked. Luca needs to marry my heir. My first born. Elena my dear. I know you weren't on board in the beginning. In fact you hated me. Hated the family for trying to force this marriage on you."

I smile up at him until a pinch on my thigh has me turning to my almost husband. "You don't hate me anymore now do you?" Luca says into my ear as he gives it a playful bite.

"Jury's still out." I reply with a straight face.

He pinches my thigh again, his hand working his way up my thigh, closer to my apex. Damn him. He's getting me riled up knowing we agreed there would be no bedroom shenanigans tonight. We were going to follow tradition and spend the last night of our single lives apart.

Luca gives a laugh. Knowing exactly where my frustrations lie. I flick my gaze to his tented pants. I'm not the only one riled up.

Together we turn our attention back to my father's speech. "Turns out. We didn't need to force a union. Luca and Elena were meant to be. Both of you were too stubborn in the beginning to admit it, but I felt it. It was love at first sight."

"More like first shot fired." Shouts Massimo. The room burst out into laughter. The events of the day I made my presence known have become a bit of a legend in the ranks of the soldiers. I give a wink to Massimo and a smile to Luca before pulling him in for a kiss.

Before our lips could meet, a series of pops went off.

Gunfire.

My father falls. "Dad!" I scream his name and try to dive for him. Luca gets to me first and pulls me to the floor. He shelters me with his body. Massimo and Val are quick to jump into action. They knock our table over while pulling out their guns.

A man can be heard laughing as the gunfire pauses. "Bosco, are you dead yet."

My eyes shoot over to my father. There is blood pouring from his arm which is being tended to by my mom. In record time she had his tie off and was using it to make a tourniquet to stop the bleeding.

"Not yet Ramirez." Replies my dad. I can tell by his face he had to work hard to keep the pain out of his voice.

"Shame. Why don't you come out from behind the table and surrender to me? I would hate to have to kill more of your family tonight. From what I hear your bloodline is near over. Give yourself up and I'll let your daughters live."

Behind the cover of our table, we each pull our weapons out. Milan hasn't learned to shoot yet. Massimo will ensure she is covered, but hands her a gun anyway. Worst case she missed. Best case, she hits one of the assholes.

Massimo is quick to show her how to turn the safety off and whispers further instructions to her. My mom has her gun pulled alongside dad and his. A quick scan around the room, or at least as much of it as I can see, shows me that the family is ready to defend themselves. And the Don. It was the way of the Caruso family.

Luca gives me a soft shake of the head. A smile teasing the corner of his lips. He knows I am making a plan in my head to end this. Ramirez is one of two final names on my list. The other is his second. Both assholes are here.

I can't waste this opportunity. Together, and as quietly as we can, we crawl across the floor. Our move is blocked by the long table. Making it to the end, I turn to glimpse around the edge. I need to know the positioning of our enemies in order to know the most effective way to attack.

Ramirez's body is blocked by a wall of his men. "Coward." I scoff.

If I can get off three to four quick shot, I could take out the men in front of him and maybe land a bullet on him. If I'm not the only one shooting I can almost guarantee I'll hit him center mass.

I turn to whisper to Luca who hasn't gotten a look at the enemy's location. He knows they are near the door. "Four guards in front. Need them down so I can take shot at Ramirez."

Luca nods to Massimo and Val. They crawl a bit closer. I repeat the number of guards to them and specify their location in regards to the door and Ramirez. Val is going to take the two on the right. Massimo will take the left. I've got Ramirez and Luca will take off after Ramirez's second, Julio, once the five men are down. The coward is keeping himself back and in position to run if things go wrong.

It's smart. But cowardly. I hate fucking cowards. The asshole dies tonight.

Without further words, I know we are all on the same page. Now we just need to make sure that no one is still shooting when Luca goes after Julio.

"I've got it." Says Milan as she crawls away from us. She moves first to Bosco and mom to relay to them. She then makes her way as close as she can to the next table. It takes only a minute for word to quietly spread around the room.

Ramirez and my dad are still locked in a debate when I lock eyes with Luca. "Love you!" He whispers to me then pecks me on the lips. I smile in return. I wanted to deepen the kiss but we have work to do. Luca moves into position. He chances a glance at the door and nods to confirm the enemy hasn't changed position.

I hold up three fingers. I lower one at a time, counting down. The moment my last finger drops. Massimo, Val, and I jump up from our position. Our guns firing rapidly as we each take down our target. The four guards fall each with two to the chest. Ramirez falls after my second shot. He's not dead. He doesn't deserve a quick death.

The Cartel is responsible for the kidnapping and sale of young girls onto the black market. It's a dark business our Mafia does not partake in. I had intended to kill him on the spot. I'm glad I didn't. The asshole would be brought to our warehouse where Luca and I could oversee the extraction of knowledge.

Only one of the guards had gotten a shot off. The bullet hit Councilmen Armano. It was only a flesh wound. He would live.

I glance around for Luca. He took off running to Julio as soon as we started firing. I wanted to go after him. Massimo and Val beat me to it. Probably for the best. They were faster than me anyway.

Instead, I made my way over to Ramirez. "You bitch!" He spits at me as he presses his good hand to his shoulder to slow the bleeding. I bet it hurts. I had shot the gun from his hand first. My bullet ripped his right hand apart. I would need a closer look but I think he is missing two fingers. My second bullet hit bone in his clavicle. It might even be shattered.

Good. The asshole deserves pain. This won't be the last either. His injuries aren't life threatening. Not yet at least.

Caruso men move around me. No doubt cleaning up the mess and disposing of the Cartel trash. A second round of men surround me. Protecting me. I don't need it. Ramirez is no longer a threat. I appreciate the sentiment anyway.

I give a nod to two of the soldiers. They are quick to pull out zip ties and rope for the scum in front of me. "Not a bitch." I pause for dramatic effect. A Queen."

I stand up and take two steps back. He is gagged, hog tied and removed. The men will see to it that he is set up in the warehouse. His wounds will be tended to, but only enough so he doesn't bleed out before we get to question him.

Luca strolls in through the front door. A massive smile on his face. Also a newly forming bruise along his jaw. From his quarrel with Julio no doubt. His return tells me Julio is dead.

He makes quick work of coming to my side. Massimo and Val aren't far behind. "My Queen." Luca says as he gives a bit of a bow. Then he grabs my hand and kisses the back of it. He turns it over and places something cold and hard in my hand. It's a necklace. A gold cross coated in blood. Julio's. It had been visible in my surveillance photos each time he met with Santo.

I throw the chain to the ground and launch myself at Luca. He catches me. His hands groping my ass. It's inappropriate for our current company but I can't get myself to care.

"Thank you!" I say as I snuggle into his chest.

"Is that it? Is your list complete?" He asks with a laugh.

I love that we can laugh about my blood thirstiness. "Yes. It's done."

"Good. Because as much fun as doling out an ass kicking is. I've never been a fan of red weddings." I laugh so hard I snort.

"No red wedding. No blood. I promise."

Luca carries me to a nearby table that is surprisingly still standing upright. He eases us down into a chair. "You sure this is the life you want? You completed your mission. You could leave now."

I put my arms around his neck and pull him close. Our foreheads rest against each other. "Can't get rid of me that easy. You'll have to marry me first." He barks out a laugh. I knew he would get my reference to my parents. It was only two weeks after they married that my mother left.

"Oh, I'll be marrying you. Then fucking you into next week." He plants kisses along my jaw as he talks. "If you run, I will chase you. And then I will fuck you again and again until you never want to leave me."

"Promise?"

"Fuck yes!" He smashes his lips to mine. Our kiss is raw and dirty. I have to keep my hands under control and remember that there are people around.

Tomorrow I can strip him naked and have my way with him.

CHAPTER TWENTY-FIVE

Luca

The music begins to play. Its soft melody bounced around the walls of the Cathedral. My hands are sweating even though I'm not nervous. Massimo and Val stand by my side as my groomsmen. I'm not nervous to marry Elena. I love her. I can't wait to see where our lives take us. What does have me sweating is the lingering thought that she might run. I don't want to believe it. I trust her when she says she is done. However there is that small part of me that has a slight hint of a doubt.

The front doors open. I hold my breath. Massimo gives a laugh beside me. "She's coming bro. Relax. She loves you." I release only half a breath. I need to see her.

Milan steps through the doors first. She walks slowly down the aisle. She is smiling brightly. A real and true smile. There is no animosity between any of us. She still has a bit of a crush on me. I see it from time to time when she looks at me. It doesn't bother me like it used to. She is opening herself up to finding someone else now. As soon as she does, she won't give me another thought.

Any man will be lucky to have her. Especially now that her ridiculous heels, tight dresses, and heavy make-up are gone. Today she wears an outfit similar to the ones she now wears daily. Elena wanted her comfortable. She wears a flowing floor length maroon gown, light make-up and her new converse sneakers. They don't go at all with the dress but Elena insisted she could wear them anyway.

When she passed by her father. Her biological father, she smiles brightly. Mario gives her a wink. I meet her at the end of the aisle and give her a kiss on the cheek. "You look beautiful Milan."

"Thank you." She grabs my hand and gives it a squeeze. "I'm happy for you Luca. Truly. We never would have worked. You needed someone stronger."

My gaze drifts over her shoulder to the open doorway. Elena isn't there. The sliver of fear creeps back up. "You'll find the person meant for you."

Milan chuckles. "You mean you'll arrange it?"

I can't help but to bark out a laugh. "We'll see." I say as I give her a kiss on the forehead. She moves to her designated spot. The music changes. Our guests packing the pews all stand. My heart speeds up. Moment of truth. Is she here or did she run?

I take a deep breath and slowly move my eyes to the door. Bosco is alone in the entryway. No. Fuck. My feet carry me two steps before Massimo grabs my shoulder and holds me back. "Give it a second." He says with a laugh. He's had a long few nights. The dark circles under his eyes are exaggerated by his smile. He hasn't complained. And he won't. He never does.

Two nights ago we got a call. A woman was seen out on Tuesday with an Irish Capo and then going home with a

Russian soldier Wednesday. On Thursday she was getting close to one of our own. She is currently locked in our basement. She refuses to talk. We don't torture woman. Not physically. We have other ways of getting them to talk, but this woman is strong. She is holding out. She reminds me of my Elena.

I gave Massimo complete control. He has my approval to do what he feels he needs to do to get the information out of her. He won't kill her. No permanent damage either. I hope.

Turning back to the door my mind returns to Elena. I begin to count.

One.

Two.

Three.

There she is. My beautiful bride steps around the corner and links her arm around Bosco's. Thank fuck! A massive smile dances on her face. The little vixen did it on purpose. She knew I would have a moment of panic.

Massimo gives my shoulder a squeeze then releases me.

Her eyes never leave mine and she makes her way down the aisle. Her father stops the two of them a step before me. I want to yank her out of his arms and pull her to me. He isn't moving fast enough for me. I need her in my arms. Bosco turns and kisses her cheek. "Love you darling." He whispers to her. I see the start of a tear in her eye before she blinks it away.

"Love you too dad". The deadly Don sheds his tears. Unlike her he doesn't blink them away. The man has no shame. Not today. Not when Elena just said she loved him in front of everyone.

He places Elena's hand in mine. Then grabs my shoulder, tightly and leans in to whisper in my ear. "You have always been like a son to me. Hurt her and she will hurt you back."

Elena hears and laughs. It's not the usual threat a father would give the groom but it fits us perfectly. "Break her heart and I will destroy you." There we go. That's the usual one.

I give him a nod and pull Elena to me. "Never. Her heart is safe with me."

"And yours with me." She replies.

Bosco leaves to take his seat by Violet. No one is around to stop me now. I grab her cheeks and pull her mouth to mine. I need her lips on mine.

"Nope." I hear Massimo shake his head more than I hear his words. "Nope none of that. You need to say I do first."

"Pussy blocker." Retorts Elena, not caring that we are standing in church just feet from the priest and with pews full of family and friends behind us. Massimo barks out a laugh. Followed by the rumblings of laughter from the entire church.

I give her a final peck on the lips and whisper in her ear, "I'll take care of your pussy later." A shiver runs down her back as we step up to the priest.

Taking a moment to reflect on the past month, I look back at Elena. Really look at her. She is happy. Finally. She has a family. Some blood, some not.

She could have run. She didn't.

Now she's mine forever.

Synopsis of Book Two: "Hunting"

Livianna

All I was trying to do was help my father.

It was supposed to be a couple of jobs.

Help him look good to the boss.

I was on the last assignment when he came hunting for me.

With a gun to my back and a needle in the neck, he took me.

Kept me in a cage, until he let me out and made me his.

Massimo

We're rounding up the last of the rats when we hear the rumors.

There's a female in the field and no one is claiming her.

She could be Irish, Russian, or Cartel.

She's certainly not one of ours.

We need to know if she's a threat before it's too late.

I'll hunt her down, lock her up, and force her to talk.

I realize, almost too late, she's not who we thought.

Now, she's in danger.

I don't need to make her mine to save her, but I will.

Also By Nova Mason

CARUSO FAMILY MAFIA
RUNNING - Luca and Elena
HUNTING - Massimo and Livianna
FIGHTING - Val and Keira

COMING SOON - DOYLE IRISH MOB
CUTTING
RIPPING
TEARING

FOLLOWED BY - VASILIEV BRATVA
CLASHING
BATTLING
WARRING

About Nova Mason

Nova Mason made her debut with her first novel "Running: Caruso Mafia Book One". The series continued with Massimo's story in "Hunting", and then Val's in "Fighting". She fell in love with books while still in the womb and learned to read at only three. Her goal as a kid was to read every book in the children's section of the local library one shelf at a time. Sadly they remodeled before she could complete her goal and lost ability to track her progress. Now she's working to fill the library in her house with books she loves and a shelf or two dedicated to her own stories.

She loves hearing from her readers, so please don't hesitate to drop her a note on one of her social media sites.

Printed in Great Britain
by Amazon

43043985R00111